Josh walked over and sat down beside her

"So what did you do with your day?" His tone was friendly, his closeness unnerving.

But Erin refused to be unnerved. "I didn't spend it in Dave's bed!" she snapped.

Josh smiled infuriatingly. "I know that. I'm still waiting for my hello kiss," he said softly.

"Then you can go—" Her protest was cut off by his mouth being placed firmly over hers. It was a kiss he intended taking full pleasure from, parting her lips with the tip of his tongue, the kiss deepening, taking on new dimensions as her mouth opened to accept the intimacy of his. Erin was dazed when at last he raised his head. "Lesson number one," he smiled.

"How did I do?" She saw his eyes widen, as if surprised by her calmness. This afternoon she had decided to accept her fate, and she would keep to that decision.

CAROLE MORTIMER
is also the author of these

Harlequin Presents

CAROLE MORTIMER

elusive lover

Harlequin Books

TORONTO • NEW YORK • LOS ANGELES • LONDON
AMSTERDAM • PARIS • SYDNEY • HAMBURG
STOCKHOLM • ATHENS • TOKYO • MILAN

Harlequin Presents first edition December 1982
ISBN 0-373-10556-8

Original hardcover edition published in 1982
by Mills & Boon Limited

CHAPTER ONE

ERIN groaned with weariness. One more room to do and she could finish for the day. So much for finishing by four-thirty! It was after that now, and as the person had checked out of this last room it was going to take at least half an hour to clean it thoroughly.

She unlocked the door, and the mess that met her gaze made her groan anew. Whoever had occupied this motel room last night had obviously thrown a party; the air was stale with cigarette smoke and empty beer bottles littered every conceivable surface.

She left the door open to clear the stale air, and started to clear the beer bottles. This room was worse than they usually were, she would never finish tonight! When Mike Johnston, the owner of the motel, had employed her two weeks ago he hadn't told her that his wife, the other cleaner, was more often out shopping than she was actually doing any work. He hadn't told her to expect constant sexual advances from him either!

It had all sounded so good—but then what wouldn't after serving greasy hamburgers in an even greasier restaurant for six weeks! Cleaning and vacuuming a few motel rooms had seemed so easy by comparison. The hours had been straight eight-thirty until four-thirty, with two clear days off a week, as a waitress she had been working shift hours, and more often than not her days off were counted as compulsory overtime. The trouble was the same thing was happening here, plus she had to fight off the advances of the men who stayed here, men who seemed to think that their rent for the night included making love to the maid in the morning.

The most recent one had been only this morning, a young boy of her own age who had tried to pull her into bed with him. Not that he hadn't been good-looking—he had; she just didn't go in for the casual sex these men expected of her.

The idea of coming to Canada had seemed so exciting—to actually visit the place where she had been born, had lived in until she was three years old, when her parents had emigrated to England. And Canada itself was lovely, especially the part of Alberta she was living in, but it was also expensive to live in Calgary, the cost of living here one of the highest in the country, and the two demanding jobs she had managed to find for herself had given her little time to go out and enjoy herself.

Mike Johnston, her boss, had offered her what he considered a form of entertainment. His form of entertainment didn't coincide with hers, and his advances were becoming more and more difficult to repulse in a joking manner, and he had implied that if she didn't soon give him what he wanted then she could start walking.

'Is this twenty-six, honey?'

Erin turned at the sound of that huskily attractive voice, the pleasant Canadian drawl she had come to love. Her eyes widened as she took in the man's appearance, the worn leather boots, the faded tight-fitting denims, the matching denim jacket worn over a red and black checked shirt, the thick black hair partly concealed by the brown cowboy hat, something a lot of Calgarian men seemed to wear, this man looked perfectly natural wearing it.

Her gaze returned to his face, a face deeply tanned, a square jaw jutting out firmly, a deep cleft in its centre, the well-shaped mouth now curved into an enquiring smile, the nose hawkish, the eyes deep-set beneath jutting dark brows, the colour of the eyes hard to distinguish from this distance, but they were definitely a light colour, blue or possibly green.

His very presence seemed to fill the shabby room, and Erin shivered with apprehension. Something about this man unnerved her. He wasn't a holidaymaker, she was sure of that, and yet he wasn't one of the rough young crowd they often had staying here either. The inability to put him into a category worried her, made her unsure of how she should act with him. He was aged about the mid-thirties mark, very good-looking in an outdoor sort of way, and surely wasn't one of those men who liked to make passes. Maybe he was in town from one of the ranches, he looked as if that sort of life——

'Well?' he tersely interrupted her thoughts, easing the holdall more comfortably on to one of his broad shoulders.

'I—er——' Erin blinked hard. 'Sorry?' she asked lamely.

He raised his eyebrows, sighing his impatience. 'Is this room twenty-six?' he repeated his first question.

'Yes,' she nodded eagerly, feeling more and more stupid by the moment, knowing she was making an idiot of herself, but unable to do anything about it.

She felt decidedly dirty in the denims and cotton top she had worn to work this morning, her blonde hair tumbling from the elastic band she secured it with while she was working, looking younger than her nineteen years with her make-up-less face and snub nose covered in freckles. She felt about fifteen, and knew she must look it too.

The man's lids lowered slightly, the lashes thick, and the colour of jet, like his overlong hair. 'Then why does it say twenty-nine on the door?' he drawled, walking inside to deposit the holdall on the unmade bed, his nose wrinkling with distaste at the mess that surrounded them.

'I—it does?' Erin frowned, walking to the door. She put up her hand to the nine and twisted it round. As soon as she took her hand away it slipped back round to the nine position. She wiped her hands nervously down her thighs. 'I think the—the screw must have fallen out,' she stated the obvious.

His mouth twisted. 'My thoughts exactly when I saw twenty-five one side and twenty-seven the other. English?' he suddenly rapped out.

'Er—yes,' she admitted huskily.

'Well, my little English miss,' he drawled mockingly, 'I happen to have rented this room for the night.'

'You have?' she asked in dismay, knowing it was going to be some time before she finished the cleaning, and she just couldn't do it under this man's watchful all-seeing gaze. She could see what colour his eyes were now; they were the deepest green she had ever seen, the colour of emeralds, a startling contrast to his deeply tanned skin.

'I have,' he confirmed tauntingly, removing his hat to reveal the darkest hair Erin had ever seen, a deep ebony, with a bluish sheen to the shine. And he was such a tall man, dwarfing her five feet two by at least a foot, his eyes narrowing as she continued to stare at him.

Erin grimaced. 'I haven't finished cleaning in here yet.'

He looked slowly around the room, not missing a bottle or a cigarette stub. 'Honey, I hope you haven't even started. I would hate to think rooms were rented out in this condition.'

She put her hand up to her untidy hair. 'I'm a—a little behind today,' she told him nervously.

He looked appreciatively at that part of her anatomy. 'You look as if you're a little behind every day,' he mocked, his gaze returning to her flushed face.

Erin just looked flustered. 'I—I meant I haven't finished my work yet.'

'I know what you meant, honey——'

'I am not your honey!' she exploded. It had been a long

day, and she was hot and tired, tired of making beds, tired of cleaning dirty bathrooms, and she wasn't in the mood to let this mocking stranger use her for his amusement. 'I'm not you anything,' she told him firmly. 'Now I'll get your room ready as soon as possible, but I'm afraid it will take a few minutes.'

'Now don't apologise, you're spoiling the whole effect.'

She frowned at him, feeling like a mouse being tormented by a cat. 'Effect?' she blinked her puzzlement.

'For a while there I thought you must have a permanent stammer,' he drawled. 'That little show of temper showed me you don't. So don't start babbling like an idiot again.' He sat down on the bed, leaning back against the headboard, his dusty, boot-clad feet on the bedcover.

Erin gasped her indignation. 'Don't call me an idiot! And get your feet off the bed!'

He smiled, revealing very white teeth. 'You haven't changed the bed yet, have you?'

'You know I haven't!'

'Then my feet stay where they are. At least this way I'll know you changed all the bed-linen.'

Her hands clenched into fists at her sides, and she could quite cheerfully have hit him in that moment, regardless of the consequences. 'I always change all the bed-linen,' she snapped.

He put his hands up behind his head and leaned back. 'Don't let me keep you from your work,' he taunted.

'You aren't!' She marched angrily into the bathroom, beginning to wash the bath in hard angry strokes. Arrogantly, mocking man! He was just what she needed at the end of a long, hard day!

'Calmed down yet?'

She turned to see him standing in the open doorway, seeming to fill most of it. 'I'm perfectly calm,' she said in her most haughty English accent.

'Mm, I can see that,' he mocked, coming to sit on the side of the bath as she moved to clean the sink.

He was overwhelming this close to, smelling of a mixture of some tangy masculine cologne or aftershave and a much more basically male smell, one that stirred the senses, one that warned you to beware of this man. Erin didn't need any warning, she could see he was dangerous!

She pointedly ignored him as she continued to clean the bathroom, which wasn't all that easy with those lazy green eyes watching her so closely. He leant casually against the doorjamb now, his arms folded across his muscular chest. Erin was aware of his every movement without even having to look at him.

She brushed past him on her way out to the main room, coming into contact with the hardness of his thighs before moving sharply away, the hot colour flooding her cheeks.

Again he followed her, sitting down on one of the double beds. 'What's a sweet little baby like you doing in a place like this?' he asked suddenly.

Erin flashed him a resentful glance. 'That isn't very original!'

His expression hardened. 'It wasn't meant to be,' he rasped. 'It was a sincere question. Little girls like you have been known to be gobbled up and never heard of again in this city.'

She could believe it; she seemed to have done nothing but fight off one man or another since she had been here— and for all of his lightly teasing manner she wasn't so sure this man's intentions were any different!

He gave her a scathing look. 'I don't happen to be "hungry" for skinny little English girls,' he taunted, seeming to read her thoughts.

She flushed fiery red. 'I'm as Canadian as you are!'

His dark eyebrows rose. 'Really?' he obviously doubted her claim.

'Yes, really.' She gave up all pretence of working, knowing she was only making a mess of it anyway. 'I was born in Calgary,' she told him with a certain feeling of triumph.

'Then why do you sound like a prissy English girl?'

Erin gasped. 'Because I was brought up a pris—I was brought up in England,' she amended at his taunting smile. Her chin went up in challenge. 'Where they obviously taught me more manners than you were ever taught in Canada!'

He gave a shout of laughter, tiny lines appearing beside his twinkling green eyes, the cleft in his chin more pronounced. 'What's your name, funny face?' he sobered.

'Erin Richards,' she revealed stiffly.

He held out his hand. 'Joshua Hawke—Josh to you.'

His hand was firm and strong, sending an electric thrill tingling up her arm and down her spine. She felt mesmerised by the warmth of those emerald-coloured eyes, then suddenly realised he hadn't released her hand, and snatched it away as if he burnt her.

She licked her suddenly dry lips. 'I—I'd rather call you Mr Hawke,' she said stiffly.

He grinned. 'I'm sure you would, hon—sweetheart, but——'

'I don't like being called sweetheart any more than I enjoy being called honey,' she cut in firmly, deciding the time had come to put this conversation on a more businesslike footing.

Joshua Hawke still grinned at her. 'You're acting prissy again,' he taunted.

She drew in an angry breath. 'And you're being rude again!'

He pursed his lips together thoughtfully. 'Okay, Erin, truce. Now, tell me how a native Calgarian talks with that precise English accent. Was that bordering on the rude again?' he quirked an eyebrow mockingly.

'You know it was!'

He sighed. 'So just tell me. The less *I* say the less chance I have of offending you.'

'I don't have the time to talk.' She began stripping the beds. 'I have to finish getting your room ready, and I work quicker if I don't talk.'

'Then I'll help you.' He marched over to her trolley and picked up the clean sheets, spreading one of them on the mattress.

'But you—you can't do that!' she gasped.

'I just did.' He calmly continued to make the bed. 'You look as if you've done enough already.' He stopped to frown at her pale cheeks and slender body. 'Do you eat?'

'Of course I eat!' she snapped her resentment.

He stood up to survey the too-slender curves below faded denims and light cotton sun-top, seeming to strip this fragile covering from her body and see the gauntness below. His eyes narrowed to steely slits. 'How often?' he demanded to know.

Not as often as she should. For one thing she didn't have the time, and for another she didn't have the money, not to eat the nourishing food that she needed anyway. French fries and hamburgers were cheap, but after cooking and serving them for six weeks she couldn't even look at them, let alone eat them.

'Well?' he rapped out.

Erin scowled at him, wishing he would just mind his own business. 'I eat as often as I'm hungry,' she evaded.

His look was considering. 'And how often is that?'

'Once, sometimes twice a day,' she admitted grudgingly.

His expression darkened. 'And did you eat today?'

'Not yet,' she mumbled, unable to meet his searching gaze. What did it have to do with *him* how often she ate!

'Are you going to?' he persisted.

'I—Probably.'

'Which means you aren't going to,' he sighed. 'How long have you been over here?'

'Eight weeks,' she frowned.

'And how much weight have you lost in that time?'

'I—'

'How much, Erin?'

'Twelve pounds,' she muttered.

He nodded, as if he had already guessed as much. 'Twelve pounds you couldn't do without.'

She glared at him. 'What does it have to do with you? What do you care that I don't eat?'

His expression softened. 'I care, Erin. I care,' he repeated gently.

It was the gentleness that was her undoing. She swallowed hard, her face suddenly crumpling, deep sobs racking her body as she cried out all the misery of the last few weeks.

'Hey, it's all right, honey!' Strong arms came about her and she was drawn against a hard chest, lean fingers gently caressing her golden locks. 'I didn't mean to upset you,' Josh Hawke's warm breath stirred the hair at her temple.

'You didn't,' she choked. 'At least, only indirectly.' She burrowed against his chest, somehow feeling safe and secure, held close in his arms, his skin smooth against her cheek where his shirt was partly unbuttoned.

'Tell me,' he encouraged softly.

Her body shuddered emotionally. 'It's just so long since—since anyone said that to me.'

'Said what, little one?' He slowly caressed her back.

Erin sniffed inelegantly. 'That they—they cared!' She started to cry once again.

His arms tightened about her. 'Cry it all out, baby,' he soothed. 'And then we can talk.'

That stopped her tears. 'T-talk?'

'Yes, talk. I want to know exactly what a baby like you is doing here on your own. You should still be in school, not acting as a slave in a second-rate motel,' his voice hardened grimly over the latter.

Erin gave a watery smile, wiping her cheeks dry as she moved away from him. 'I left school years ago,' she sniffed.

'How many?'

'Three.'

'Three!' he scorned.

Her eyes widened. 'Don't you believe me?'

'No.'

She spluttered with laughter. 'You're honest, anyway.'

'That's better,' he grinned. 'You're really cute when you laugh.'

She pulled a face. 'Cute!'

'Pretty?'

'Well . . .'

'Ravishingly beautiful,' he mocked.

Erin laughed again. 'I'll stick with pretty. And I did leave school three years ago—I'm nineteen.'

'Wow!'

She flushed. 'Just because you're old——'

'I resent that, young lady,' he firmly grasped her arms. 'I'm thirty-four, and I wouldn't be nineteen again for a million dollars.'

'It's pretty rough, isn't it?' she agreed ruefully, feeling strangely breathless close to him like this, and strangely happy for the first time in months.

'It's lousy,' he nodded, glancing down at his wrist-watch. 'Hell, it's after five already.' He looked up at her. 'I have to be somewhere by six. Can we talk when I get back?'

She shrugged out of his hold on her. 'We've already talked. I—I'm sorry I cried all over your shirt. I have to go now, I should have finished hours ago.'

'Erin——'

She turned away. 'You've been very kind, Mr Hawke. I don't usually bore the guests with my problems——'

He swung her round angrily. 'I know that, damn you! Erin, I wasn't giving you the brush-off, I really do have to be somewhere by six. But I want to see you when I get back.'

'I won't be here.' She refused to look at him, feeling embarrassed at the way she had broken down in front of him. She didn't usually cry all over perfect strangers. But he was the first person to show her any real kindness since she had come to Canada, so he had been treated to all the emotion that had been building up in her over the last few weeks.

'Where will you be?' he wanted to know.

'At my home,' she answered evasively.

'Where is it?'

Her stance became defensive. 'That's none of your business. Look, I've apologised for bothering you, now would you please go on to your appointment and let me finish up here.'

'Erin, I want——'

'I don't care what you want!' She shook off his hand on her arm, running to the door. 'I'll finish your room once you've left.' She closed the door behind her and ran hurriedly to the store-room.

'Erin!' Joshua Hawke caught up with her before she reached it, spinning her round to face him. 'Now I intend talking to you.' His expression was grim, all of the lazy charm he had first teased her with completely erased. 'If you won't tell me where you live then meet me here. We can have dinner together, and you can tell me about yourself.'

She faced him defiantly. 'And why should you want to know anything about me? Haven't I told you enough— bored you enough, already?'

'You haven't bored me,' he shook her roughly. 'You're lost and alone, and——'

'But I'm not suicidal!' she scorned him.

He seemed to go pale. 'All right, Erin,' he thrust her away from him, 'if that's the way you want it.' He turned and strode off, getting into a brown pick-up, its paintwork mud-spattered, a huge wooden crate in the back. Her last glimpse of him was a narrow-eyed man intent on the road in front of him, his hat pulled low over his face, his jaw set in a firm line.

Oh, how could she have told him all those things, cried all over him like that! She just hoped she never had to face him again. She had made an absolute fool of herself.

She tidied his room so fast it must have been a record, terrified he would get back before she had finished. But he didn't, and she was able to make her escape without making any more of an idiot of herself.

Only Mike was in the office when she went in to say goodnight; Frances was probably in the back doing her nails. What else would she be doing! A curvaceous blonde of about thirty, she wasn't exactly maid material.

Mike looked up from his newspaper. 'A little late tonight, aren't you?' he scowled, a tall sandy-haired man who couldn't believe every woman he came into contact with didn't find him madly attractive. He and Frances made a good couple, although Erin wondered when they ever had time for each other, they seemed to have such a lot of other—interests.

She gave a dismissive shrug. 'I had a lot to do,' she told him pointedly.

His gaze slowly undressed her. 'So I saw,' he sneered. 'Flirting with the guests isn't what you're paid to do.'

She bit her lip. 'Flirting . . .?'

'I saw you with the Hawke guy. Find him attractive, do you?'

'I—No! No, I——'

'Liar!' he accused angrily. 'I hope you aren't up to anything with him, Erin, because I don't allow that sort of thing in my place.'

She stiffened with indignation. 'I've no intention of "getting up to anything" with Mr Hawke. I happened to be doing his room, and——'

'Spare me the details,' Mike cut in nastily. 'I just want you to remember,' he moved closer to her, his hand touching her waist, 'that I'm first in line when you do decide to start coming across.'

His crudeness made her feel sick, as did the way he was touching her. He had also answered her curiosity about Frances; she couldn't be back yet, Mike would never act this way within hearing distance of his wife.

Erin moved away from him. 'I just came in to tell you I've finished for the day. I'm going to my room now.'

His gaze ran over her suggestively. 'Want me to come with you?' he asked softly.

She swallowed hard. 'No, thank you.'

'So polite,' he taunted. 'Do you say thank you afterwards too?'

She had to get out of here, before she was physically sick. 'I—Goodnight, Mike.'

' 'Night, Erin. Tomorrow's another day, hmm?'

She looked away. 'Yes,' she agreed in a choked voice.

His mocking laughter followed her. He had her trapped, and he knew it. If only she hadn't been so stupid, so trusting. When Mike had told her that there was a room she could rent from him she had jumped at the chance of leaving the flat she had been paying an exorbitant rent for and moving in here. The room had turned out to be little more than a cupboard, the rent almost as high as the one she had been paying, also Mike conveniently had a key to her room. She had changed the lock once, but he had demanded her spare key—for fire purposes, he said. She could hardly refuse in the circumstances, and so now she lived in dread of him just letting himself into her room one night.

So far he hadn't done so, seeming to be biding his time, but she knew that very soon her time was going to run out. And she lived in dread of that day!

No wonder she had lost twelve pounds; she was surprised she hadn't lost more, having no appetite, and hardly daring to sleep at night because of Mike and that spare key.

She studied herself in the mirror once she reached her room. She looked a mess—too thin, too pale, and worst of all, no vitality. It was hard to believe this was the same näive girl who had set out so hopefully eight weeks ago.

It had taken just two weeks of that time for her to realise her father didn't want her around, another week to realise it was going to take forever to get the return air-fare together. So far she had a hundred dollars towards it, at this rate she might get back to England in six months or so.

She groaned, burying her face in the pillow and sobbing what few tears she had left after crying in Joshua Hawke's arms.

Six months ago it had all seemed so easy, so very easy. She had hardly been able to believe it when Bob had offered to buy her an air ticket to see the father who had returned to Canada when Erin was only five years old. Until she saw it was a one-way ticket!

Her mother had died just over a year ago, leaving Erin to care for the man who had been her stepfather since she was eight years old. It was the age-old story of immigrants, one partner liked the new country and one didn't. Her mother liked England and so she stayed, her father hated the little country that would fit into one corner of Canada, so he returned to his native country. They had divorced two years later, and a year after that her mother had brought Bob Walker home as her stepfather.

He wasn't the sort of man to tolerate children, liking to go out in the evenings, taking her mother with him, and so for the most part he ignored Erin's very existence. Her mother had claimed he needed time to adjust, and yet when her mother had died just after Erin's eighteenth birthday Bob was still resenting her presence in his home.

She had tried to care for Bob the way her mother had, had tried to love him, and yet it was so hard to love someone who had never shown her even one gesture of affection in the whole of the ten years she had known him.

After a year of cooking and cleaning for him, with not one word of gratitude, she was prepared to admit defeat. Then out of the blue Bob had given her the air-ticket to come out here and visit her father. She hadn't thought twice about it, writing to let her father know, and even though she had received no reply from him she had still come, sure that after all this time he would want to see her.

He hadn't. He had remarried himself, had a new family, a son and daughter of ten and eleven respectively, and his second wife had left Erin in no doubt of her opinion of her turning up on their doorstep uninvited.

Nevertheless, her father had grudgingly allowed her to stay, putting her in with Ronnie, his other daughter. Ronnie turned out to be a precocious little brat, who took every opportunity she could to let Erin know she wasn't wanted there.

The last straw had come after she had heard her father and stepmother arguing about her. With a few cruel words she had learnt that her father was no more pleased to see her than her stepmother was, that she had been the result of an effort on her parents' part to try and make their marriage work.

Even now she didn't like to think about it, to realise that

she hadn't so much been wanted by her parents but had been a final attempt to pull their marriage together. It wasn't surprising that such parents should have destroyed her.

Oh, her mother had tried her best, had loved her in her own way, but ultimately it was Bob who always came first, even if he wasn't always right.

She had left her father's house after hearing that argument, and the lack of argument at her decision to leave only served to enhance the fact that she hadn't been wanted there in the first place.

And so she had been left alone, with very little money, and no visible means of supporting herself. In a place as large as Calgary, a city growing at a rate too fast for its population, she had felt sure she would be able to get a job. She could, if she didn't mind waiting two or three weeks to get an interview. She had been through it all before in England, and she didn't have the funds to wait that long, so she took the first job she could start immediately, little realising that once she began work she had no time to look for a more suitable job.

She spent the evening doing her laundry, suddenly realising at bedtime that she hadn't eaten again. Joshua Hawke had probably gone out and had a big juicy steak, forgetting all about the childish creature he had invited to join him.

Why had he done that? He didn't seem to be the type good Samaritans were made of. And yet he had listened as she sobbed her heart out. Listened! The poor man hadn't had much choice about it, she had cried all over him!

Well, that wouldn't happen again. She didn't need or want anyone worrying over her, least of all a tall arrogant stranger who mocked her most of the time.

She didn't know whether she was relieved or disappointed when she left her room the next morning to find the brown pick-up noticeably absent. Joshua Hawke must have left very early, it was only eight-thirty now. Perhaps he worked on one of the ranches after all. But his hand, when he had touched her, hadn't felt calloused and rough. It hadn't felt soft and effeminate either, making his occupation a puzzle.

Why on earth did she keep thinking of the man! She wasn't likely to see or hear from him again, he had probably forgotten all about her now that he had returned home.

Did he have a wife? She somehow didn't think so. Why she thought that she didn't know, he just hadn't *looked* married. She was probably wrong, he probably had half a dozen children too! Maybe that was the reason he had been so patient with her display of tears, because he had children of his own.

But he hadn't treated her like a child, despite calling her 'little one' and 'baby'!

She had to stop thinking about the man; he had gone now, and she doubted he would ever be back. This motel rarely had the same visitors twice, the rooms were not exactly of a glamorous standard.

'Daydreaming?' Frances Johnston asked waspishly, as she sat behind the desk in the reception area, looking attractive in a tight blouse and even tighter skirt.

'No, I—I was just—thinking.' About Joshua Hawke! And she wouldn't do it again. The man had shown her a little kindness, but he was gone now, for ever.

Frances' mouth twisted. 'A bit early in the day for that, isn't it?'

'Maybe,' Erin dismissed, knowing that the other woman was spoiling for an argument. Frances didn't like her, was aware of her husband's interest in her, and she liked that even less. If only she knew how Erin hated Mike's attentions, the way he took every opportunity to touch her, the

way he crudely made verbal passes at her! The whole
thing made her cringe, but Frances seemed to enjoy acting
the jealous wife, and took delight in making digs at Erin
whenever they were alone together.

Frances looked down her nose at her. 'I have to take
care of the office for a couple of hours. You start the rooms
and I'll catch you up later.'

She knew that meant she was on her own again today,
and the thought of cleaning forty rooms single-handed for
the second day running made her groan in dismay.

Her resentment burned all the time she was loading the
clean linen on to the trolley, wheeling the huge vacuum-
cleaner out on to the pathway.

She couldn't stand much more of this, she just didn't
have the stamina for it. For about the tenth time in as
many days she promised herself that tonight she would
look through the newspapers for another job, knowing
that when the time came she would be too tired and dis-
heartened to bother.

Room twenty-six first; she could be sure that room was
empty. Would Joshua Hawke have left any of his personality in the room, or would it just be the impersonal
room it had always seemed?

Joshua Hawke again! He meant nothing to her, nothing.
How could she possibly miss a person she didn't even know,
a person who had taken a few minutes out of his day to
listen to her? She couldn't. And yet his mocking kindness
had stayed with her all during the night, and for once she
had slept soundlessly.

The room was in darkness, the curtains having been left
drawn, and the smell of alcohol was very strong. Erin's
nose wrinkled with distaste. Joshua Hawke hadn't just left
an imprint of his personality on the room, he had left it in
almost as much of a mess as it had been yesterday!

She sighed heavily. So he hadn't been so different after

all, just another man out for a good time. The 'talk' he
had wanted last night could have been a lot more than
that. Thank heavens she had refused.

She moved to the window to pull back the curtains and
let in some light, gasping as a hand caught her around the
wrist and the rumpled mound of sheets and blankets
materialised into a body—a male body.

'Mr Hawke!' she gasped.

' 'Morning, sweetheart,' he smiled up at her, his eyes
lazily appreciative, his black hair tousled into disorder.
The sheet fell back to his waist as he sat up in the bed, and
Erin didn't need much imagination to know that the rest
of him was as naked as that hard-muscled chest!

CHAPTER TWO

'I—Good morning,' she returned stiltedly. 'I'm sorry if I disturbed you.' She looked away from that naked chest and the clear outline of his thighs beneath the sheet.

Heavy lids lowered over teasing green eyes. 'Honey, this sort of disturbance I like,' he grinned at her.

Erin wished he wouldn't smile at her, it gave her a fluttering sensation in her stomach and made her breath catch in her throat. 'I thought this room was empty,' she said awkwardly.

'It is—except for me.'

'I——' She suddenly realised he was still holding her wrist, his thumb running over the delicate veins there. When she tried to pull away his grip tightened, pulling her down beside him on the bed. 'Would you let go of me? Please,' she added in a pleading tone.

'In a minute,' he dismissed, his other hand coming up to slowly trail the fingers down her cheek. He frowned as she flinched. 'What is it?' he asked sharply. 'Did I hurt you?'

He had been infinitely gentle, and he knew it. It was that she no longer trusted herself to be any sort of judge of character. Yesterday she had thought him a nice man who was genuinely interested in her, until he had shown her that his appointment, which by the odour in this room had been with a beer bottle, was more important than listening to the woeful tale of some unknown English girl, and now he had pulled her down on to his bed, in which he was obviously naked.

'Erin?' he prompted.

At least he remembered her name! 'No,' she moved

away from that caressing hand, 'you didn't hurt me. I'll come back when you've gone,' and she stood up, trying to pull her wrist out of his grasp.

He was completely alert now, the last blanket of sleep—or hangover—pushed to the background. 'Did you eat last night?' he asked suddenly, refusing to let her go.

He completely threw her with the unexpectedness of the question. 'No,' she answered huskily.

His face darkened with anger. 'Why?'

'I—I forgot.'

'You forgot!' he repeated in disgust. 'How can you *forget* to eat?'

Erin moved uncomfortably. 'I don't know how, I just do it all the time.'

He gave an angry sigh. 'Because you're too damn tired to think straight. What time did you finish here last night?'

'About six-thirty.'

'Plenty of time for you to have met me for dinner.'

Her nose wrinkled. 'I'd rather have no dinner at all than one that consisted mainly of beer.'

For a moment Joshua Hawke looked incredulous, then his eyes glittered with anger. 'You little——!' He broke off, pulling her roughly down beside him to bend over her, his mouth coming down savagely on hers.

Erin was shocked into acquiescence, lying quietly beneath him as he plundered her mouth with ruthless insistence, holding her arms at her sides as she began to fight him. She was suffocating, unable to breathe, and her frightened groans of distress finally seemed to reach him as he lifted his head to look down at her.

She couldn't have known the vulnerable figure she looked, with her wide frightened eyes and trembling lower lip. Joshua Hawke's expression softened as he looked down at her. 'Your accusations were unfounded, little one,' he said softly. 'But I don't think you deserved that,' he touched her slightly swollen lips. 'Do you accept my apology?'

She couldn't speak, couldn't move. 'I—I——'

'You're babbling again,' he taunted.

Her eyes flashed. 'Of course I'm babbling!' She pushed against him, the warmth of his skin seeming to burn her hand, bringing her to an awareness of the fact that only a thin cotton sheet separated her from his nakedness. She sat up, scrambling hastily off the bed. 'You shouldn't have kissed me,' she accused.

He leant back against the headboard. 'I agree, I shouldn't. But then you shouldn't have accused me of having a drinking dinner. I had a couple of beers with some friends of mine, but I certainly wasn't drunk.'

'No?' She picked a pair of crumpled denims up from the floor, giving him a pointed look before putting them on the chair.

'Don't do that!' He threw back the sheet and got out of bed, wearing a pair of navy blue briefs, his legs as tanned as the rest of him. He put the denims back on the floor. 'They happen to reek of beer.' He unzipped the holdall and pulled out another pair of denims.

Erin looked down at the floor, never having seen a man almost naked before, especially one who was so un-concerned by the fact. She daren't look up, her embarrass-ment was so acute.

'And it wasn't beer I intended drinking.' He pulled on the denims and zipped them up. 'Dave tipped a whole glassful of his beer over me—accidentally. You can look up now,' he drawled mockingly.

She looked up and then looked hastily away again. His chest was still bare, covered with a fine mat of black hair, his stomach taut and flat, the dark hair passing over his stomach, and lower. He had a magnificent body, lean and tautly muscled, and just to look at him made her blush.

His hand came up under her chin to tilt her face up to him, forcing her to look at him. 'Hey, no one is that shy,' he teased.

'I am!' she snapped. 'Put it down to my prissy English background,' she added bitchily.

He laughed. 'I'm not to be forgiven for that either, hmm?'

She sighed. 'I just wish you wouldn't tease me.'

His thumb slowly caressed her bottom lip. 'Who says I was teasing?'

Her eyes flew open, deeply blue, her lashes long and thick, naturally so. 'I—You must have been,' she fluttered.

He raised his eyebrows. 'Must I?'

'Yes . . .'

Josh Hawke shook his head. 'I never tease when I make love to a woman. But you're such a baby, I probably scared the hell out of you, hmm?'

She licked her lips nervously. 'A—a bit.'

He nodded. 'I thought so. Well, this time I'm forewarning you. You have two seconds to move away, otherwise I'm going to kiss you again.'

She couldn't move; she tried, but something held her back. Maybe it was the warmth of his breath against her cheek, or the mesmerism of his deep green eyes, whatever the reason she hadn't moved when his head lowered to claim her lips for the second time.

His shoulders felt firm beneath her touch as he curved her slender body against the hardness of his, almost lifting her off the ground as he held her to him. His mouth moved druggingly against her, his hands moving down her back, his fingertips running lightly up and down her spine.

Erin was starving for affection, crying out for someone to love her. It had been so long since anyone had held her, kissed her, and she fell a victim of her own weakness for affection, her arms entwining about his neck as she stood on tiptoe to increase the pressure of his mouth on hers.

He pulled back with a gasp. 'Erin——'

'Yes—Erin,' drawled a sarcastic voice from the doorway.

She turned a guilt-stricken face to Frances Johnston as she stood in the doorway, pulling out of Josh Hawke's arms to run to the door, brushing past Frances and out of the room.

'Erin——'

'Don't worry about her,' Frances softly interrupted Josh as he came after Erin, and her hand glided up his chest, her long nails painted a deep dark red, 'Erin tends to be a little—emotional,' she added huskily. 'Youth has a way of looking at these things differently.'

Erin turned just in time to see Frances moving insinuatingly against Josh as she slowly pushed him back inside the room.

She couldn't stay here another moment longer, she just couldn't. She might be left out on a limb, with no job and nowhere to sleep, but after what Frances had just witnessed her life wouldn't be worth living around here anyway.

Once she reached the privacy of her room she threw all her belongings into her battered suitcase, tears streaming down her face. Josh was probably reaping the benefit of Frances' experience at this moment. He would certainly find she had a lot more to offer than Erin had.

God, she hated him, hated them both. How could she have let Josh kiss her like that, have actually kissed him back! It wouldn't have happened normally, not if she weren't feeling so miserably alone. She wasn't usually susceptible to the lazy charm Josh had seduced her with, she was just homesick, needed to get back to England, to——

Who was she kidding? The man had enough charm and sexual attraction to make her fall for the same thing all over again. He had probably recognised her need for some kind of human warmth, and had decided to take advantage of it.

She was such a fool, such a complete and utter idiot. A man like that wouldn't seriously be interested in someone like her. He was in town looking for fun—and she was supposed to be *it*. Frances would be a willing stand-in, and Joshua Hawke would probably enjoy it more with her.

The door to her room was suddenly flung open, and Mike Johnston came inside and closed the door. 'Well, well, well,' he taunted, his gaze insolently undressing her. 'And just where do you think you're going?' he looked pointedly at her half packed suitcase.

She threw some more clothes inside, not caring that they would all be creased and unwearable when next she opened it. 'I'm leaving,' she threw some more things in the case. 'Right now.'

'Oh yeah?' he sneered, his arms folded challengingly across his chest.

'Yes,' she nodded, going into the bathroom to collect her few cosmetics.

Mike followed her, swinging her round to face him. 'You can't just walk out on me.'

'I'm going!' She tried to pry his fingers from her arm, but they refused to be dislodged. 'Let me go, Mike.'

'Not until you've given me what I want, what you gave that guy in room twenty-six last night.' His wet lips came down on hers, forcing her head back, her arms twisted painfully behind her back.

'No!' She wrenched her mouth away, struggling to be free.

'Yes!' he hissed, pulling her so hard against him that he knocked the breath from her body, momentarily dazing her. He pushed her over to the bed and forced her down, his weight pressing down on her.

After Josh this man was grotesque, everything about him nauseating her, so much so that she couldn't even fight him as he pulled her shirt out of her denims and roughly undid the buttons.

'I told you I was the first in line when you started coming across,' he breathed heavily as he looked down at her nakedness. 'Frances told me you stayed with that guy Hawke last night,' he snarled.

That brought her out of her daze. 'Frances told you . . .?'

'Just now,' he nodded, his mouth plundering the hollow between her breasts.

Just now? That meant Frances must have left Josh almost immediately, and from the way she had made a play for him Erin didn't think the other woman had been the one to call a halt. Josh must have rejected her, he must have done!

She began to struggle now, to fight back, although she didn't give herself time to wonder why Josh's lack of interest in Frances should cause this reaction. 'Let me go, Mike,' she ordered firmly. 'Let me go!' she panicked as he refused to be pushed off, his weight heavy on top of her.

Suddenly he was pulled off her and slammed against the wall. 'You heard the lady,' Josh told him, dangerously soft, his eyes glittering like green pebbles as he held the other man pinned to the wall. 'She doesn't like you touching her.'

Erin was too busy rebuttoning her shirt to care about the damage Josh might do to Mike; the former was obviously the stronger and fitter of the two.

Mike gave a taunting smile, holding up his hands defensively. 'She's all yours, if you want her badly enough to fight over her. Personally I've never found her that good.'

She gasped. 'Why, you——'

'Keep your dirty comments to yourself,' Josh rasped, his

grasp tightening about the other man's throat. 'Or would you like me to make you?'

'Josh——'

'You can get out,' Mike turned on her savagely. 'Just take your things and get out.'

'Don't worry,' Josh's mouth twisted, 'I don't intend leaving her here with you.' He thrust the other man away from him, wiping his hands down his denim-clad thighs, as if the touch of the other man had contaminated him.

'Why, you——!' Mike raised a fist and swung it at Josh, missing by inches as the latter ducked, his own fist landing painfully in Mike's flabby stomach. 'Hell!' Mike groaned, bent over double.

'Get out,' Josh ordered coldly.

Mike looked up with jaundiced eyes. 'You can't tell me to get out of my own property!'

'I just did.'

'But——'

'Out!' Josh snapped tautly.

Mike staggered to the door. 'I meant it about your going,' he snarled at Erin's bent head.

'Neither of us will be staying,' Josh answered for her. 'As soon as Erin has her things together we'll both be leaving.'

'That will save me the trouble of throwing you out!' Even Mike must have realised that was a purely defensive threat, because he made a hasty exit.

Erin slumped back down on to the rumpled bed. 'Oh, God!' she shuddered, burying her face in her hands.

Josh's arm came about her shoulders as he sat down next to her. 'It's all over now, sweetheart,' he comforted gently.

She stiffened, moving away from him. 'Until the next time,' she mumbled, standing up to fasten her packed suitcase.

His eyes narrowed to steely green slits. 'What's that supposed to mean?'

She shrugged, feeling cold inside, numb. 'Men are all the same—they take, they don't give.'

Amusement lightened his expression. 'And where did you learn that little gem?'

Her eyes sparkled as she glared at him. 'From men like you, like Mike, like—like——'

'Like?' he suddenly towered over her.

'Like my father, like Bob,' she told him vehemently. 'My father only had me in the first place to try and keep his marriage together, and when it didn't he couldn't give a damn about me. And as for Bob, he never wanted me in the first place. He couldn't wait to throw me out either.'

'What did you do to him?' Josh drawled.

'Nothing! I tried to do everything for him. I took care of him, I even tried to love him, and in the end he threw me out. He has a woman called Mary living with him now,' she added bitterly.

She had written to Bob to let him know she was leaving her father's house, and he had written back telling her that there was no place for her at his home, that he had a girl-friend, a girl-friend who had moved in with him. She hadn't been in touch with him since.

'Are you ready to leave?' Josh asked abruptly.

'Yes. But I don't really expect you to leave with me.' She shrugged. 'Why should you?'

'Maybe I don't like the idea of the barracuda being able to enter my room any time she chooses. Or maybe I just don't like the idea of that guy trying to get into bed with the girls who work for him.'

'Girl,' Erin corrected, pulling on her jacket. 'I'm the only girl who works for him,' she explained at his questioning look.

'And the barracuda?'

'Mike's wife, Frances.'

The green eyes widened. 'Those two are married?'

Her mouth twisted wryly. 'I'm afraid so.'

'Hell,' Josh shook his head. 'Do they have any children?'

'No—thank God.'

'My sentiments exactly.' He buttoned the shirt he had obviously pulled on in a hurry. 'Do you know that woman was perfectly willing to carry on where you'd left off?' he expressed his disgust.

Colour flooded her cheeks as she remembered exactly where she had 'left off'. 'You aren't telling me you didn't like it,' she scorned to hide her embarrassment.

His expression darkened, his handsome face harsh. 'Would I be here if I did?'

'I—No, I suppose not.'

'Definitely not.' His mouth twisted. 'Now let's get going. I'll take you out to breakfast.'

'I'm not——'

'You're eating,' he told her firmly, pulling her out of the room with him. 'I'll just get my holdall. Wait here for me,' he instructed once they reached the front of the motel.

Erin waited until he had entered his room before going into the reception area. Frances wasn't there, so perhaps she was actually cleaning the rooms for a change. After all, there was no one else to do it, not now.

Mike looked up with a scowl; his stomach was obviously still bothering him. 'What do you want?' he growled.

Erin stood her ground, sick of being exploited, determined not to take it any more. 'I want my wages for the past week,' she told him unflinchingly.

His face became flushed with anger. 'You have to be kidding,' he scoffed, his gaze insolent. 'Let your lover take care of you.'

She had to bite her tongue to stop the fiery retort that

sprang to her lips. She wouldn't give this man the satisfac-
tion of losing her temper with him, he just wasn't worth it.
'I want my wages,' she repeated in a controlled voice.
'And I want them now.'

'Well, you aren't getting them,' he told her nastily.

'Is that your last word on the subject?'

'Yes, that's my last word on the subject,' he mimicked.

'Very well,' she gave a cold inclination of her head,
'you'll be hearing from my lawyer.'

His eyes widened in surprise. 'Over a few dollars?'

Erin shook her head, remaining calm and composed. It
was as if she were someone else, a new Erin who wouldn't
be undermined. 'Not over a few dollars, no. But over a
case of sexual harassment, yes.'

He gasped. 'Sexual harassment——! My God, you little
bitch!'

'I mean it,' she said firmly.

He was white with anger. 'I can see that, damn you,' he
rasped, pulling open a drawer to take out some dollars and
throw them across the desk at her. 'Here, take it. And
don't ever come back.'

'I don't intend to.' Erin picked up the money and
crammed it into her denims pocket, picked up her suitcase
and turned to leave. Josh was leaning against the doorjamb, open respect in the warmth of his eyes. 'Thank you,'
she accepted gratefully as he took her suitcase out of her
shaking hand.

'You took a risk in there, little one,' he said once they
were outside, his expression grim. 'He could have got really
nasty.'

'So could I,' she told him without emotion.

Josh shook his head. 'Not as nasty as he could. I thought
you'd left, you know,' he gave her a sideways glance.

If she could have got her money and left before he
reappeared then she probably would have done. As it was

she intended taking the first opportunity she could to get away from him. She had had it with men, any man.

'Not until I had my money,' she said firmly.

'You said sexual harassment,' he recalled slowly. 'Does that mean this morning has happened before?'

She flushed. 'Not in such intensity, no. Could you slow down a little?' she requested impatiently, having great difficulty keeping up with his longer strides. 'Where's your pick-up truck, anyway?'

'Being serviced. It should be ready this afternoon.' He slowed down. 'What do you mean, not in such intensity?'

She shot him a resentful glance, once again acknowledging, reluctantly, how well the hat, denims, and boots suited his dark, rugged attractiveness. He could almost have belonged to the days of the Wild West, almost. But there was an air of awareness about him, almost one of sophistication—if it could be called that, an impression of worldliness that seemed to indicate that he didn't always dress or act this casually.

'Erin?' he prompted at her silence.

'Oh, he just—he's touched me, made implications, things like that,' she dismissed, hating having to talk about such things, especially to the man she had kissed so passionately only minutes earlier. 'Nothing I couldn't handle.'

'Until this morning,' he said dryly.

'That was your fault,' she flashed. 'Oh yes, it was,' she insisted at his sceptical snort. 'Frances told Mike that you and I had spent the night together. He didn't like that.'

'It seems the barracuda can talk when she wants to. It took me a hell of a long time to get her to tell me where you were living,' he explained. 'Did that guy force his way into your room just now?'

'Or did I let him in, you mean?' she scorned bitterly.

'No, I didn't mean.' His expression darkened. 'How did

he get in if you didn't let him in?'

'By using his key,' she revealed dully.

'You gave him——'

'No, I didn't!' she snapped, and explained how Mike came to have a key to her room.

'The bastard!' Josh muttered.

'Yes.' They were still walking, apparently with no purpose in mind. 'Where are we going?'

'I told you, to have breakfast. Here we are,' he stopped outside one of the restaurants she never seemed to have the time to try. 'I hope you're hungry,' he said before going inside.

Erin had the feeling that even if she weren't he would still make sure she ate. She had no choice but to follow him in, her case, with all her worldly possessions, still held firmly in his hand.

He was greeted like a regular, obviously well known by the waitress who came to seat them. 'Table for two, Josh?' she looked speculatively at Erin.

And no wonder! It was only nine-thirty in the morning, and Josh was still carrying her suitcase.

'That's right, Marie,' he grinned at the young girl, her open, fresh prettiness obviously appealing to him. 'And do you have somewhere to stow this until after we've eaten?' he indicated the suitcase.

'Sure——'

'Oh, but——'

'Something wrong, Erin?' Josh quirked one black eyebrow at her.

She reached for the case, anxious not to let it out of her sight. 'I'd rather keep it with me.' It was all she had in the world.

'Okay,' but he kept a firm grip on it. 'Table for two people and a suitcase, Marie,' he requested tauntingly.

Erin waited until the other girl had poured their coffee

before lashing out at him. 'It's all right for you to laugh at me,' she snapped, 'but everything I own is in that case.'

He pulled a face. 'It doesn't weigh much.'

'That's because I don't own much!'

'Drink your coffee,' he instructed. 'It's good and strong. You'll feel better for it.'

'How do you know that?' she asked in a disgruntled voice. 'I may not even like coffee. Did that occur to you when you were accepting on my behalf?'

'You should have said——'

'As it happens, I like coffee,' she told him coldly. 'What I *don't* like is someone making my mind up for me.'

Green eyes narrowed with impatience. 'I'm sorry, Your Majesty. Is this place to your liking, Your Highness?'

She blushed at his sarcasm, pretending to look around consideringly. Compared to the eating-house she had worked in this was really good, very clean, the booths and tables all fitted out in green crushed velvet, the staff all smartly dressed in black and white.

The two of them were seated in a side booth, the hot sun from outside not filtering through the small set-back window and so making it hot and uncomfortable to eat.

'Well?' Josh prompted.

Erin looked back at him. He was easily the most attractive man in the room; most of the other tables were full. He had taken off his hat now that they were inside, and his hair appeared even blacker, slightly ruffled where he had run a casual hand through it. The denim jacket and trousers were just as casual, the boots just as dusty, and yet he stood out from the similarly clad men in the room.

'It's all right,' she shrugged, annoyed with herself for noticing how attractive Josh was. Enough men had hurt her lately, without her falling for this man.

Marie came back to take their order, and Erin half-heartedly ordered eggs and bacon, making sure her request

for her eggs to be 'flipped over' went in, the thought of the
near raw eggs she would be served if it didn't making her
feel nauseous. She had made that mistake once, but she
had never made it again. Josh ordered everything—eggs,
bacon, sausages, and wheatcakes.

'Like some?' he asked as he requested the latter.

'No, thank you,' she grimaced. She would have enough
trouble getting the eggs and bacon down her. Since she
had stopped eating so much she had been unable to take
in great amounts when she did get around to having a
meal.

'Hash browns?' he asked hopefully.

She rather liked this form of fried potato, so she nodded
acceptance. 'Please,' she added politely, sitting back as her
coffee cup was refilled. She had learnt that wherever you
went they would just keep filling your cup up with coffee
unless you asked them to stop, and they never seemed to
charge any more for it. She knew, because sometimes these
gallons of coffee were all she could afford on the budget
she had allowed herself.

'At last we've found something the lady likes,' Josh
taunted, sitting back in his seat as he watched her through
narrowed eyes.

Erin flushed. 'I'm sorry if I'm bad company. It isn't
every day I lose my job and get thrown out of my lodg-
ings.'

'Mm, we'll have to see what we can do about that later.
Right now I intend to have that talk you vetoed last night.
Let's start at the beginning. How did you get out here in
the first place?'

'Plane!' she mocked.

'Very funny! I meant where did you get the money
from?'

It must be obvious from her clothes that she couldn't
have afforded the ticket herself, and she flushed her resent-

ment. 'How do you think I got it? Walking the streets?'

Josh sat forward with a sigh, obviously coming to the end of his patience with her. 'You tell me,' he drawled. 'Did you?'

'Of course not——'

'Why so indignant, Erin? You brought the subject up, I'm just asking. Is that the way you got your money together to come here?'

He was serious, damn him! Her sarcasm had backfired on her, Josh's intent look showed her that he wanted an answer. 'No, it isn't! Bob bought me a one-way ticket.'

'Boy, he must have really wanted to get rid of you. Not a very good reference, is it?' Josh mocked.

Erin gave him a startled look. 'I beg your pardon?'

'It doesn't matter,' he dismissed. 'You aren't bad at keeping a place clean, anyway.'

She flushed. 'I'll get another job, if that's what you mean.'

'Honey, I'm sure you will. With your talents you're sure to be in demand.'

'If you're being sarcastic——'

'Oh, but I'm not. I know a lot of men who would jump at the chance of having someone like you to keep their house clean during the day and their bed warm at night.'

'You——'

'Our breakfast has arrived, Erin,' he interrupted what looked like being a tirade, sitting back while his laden plate was placed in front of him, smiling up at the susceptible Marie.

Erin saw that smile, and the effect it had on the other girl, and looked away. One smile and he thought he had Marie in the palm of his hand. Maybe he did, but his charm wasn't working as well on her. She would just have her breakfast and go, knowing she had to find herself another job before this evening or risk sleeping under the stars. She had no idea how the police felt about people sleeping out on benches over here; in London they were usually moved on or arrested for the night. That would be all she needed!

She thanked Marie for bringing her meal. 'I don't like the implications of your remark,' she told Josh once the waitress had moved away.

He looked up from pouring maple syrup on his wheatcakes. 'I wasn't implying anything, I was stating a fact. On your track record you're sure to get yourself into another unwanted situation.'

'I didn't choose to have Mike makes passes at me!' Her eyes flashed deeply violet.

'Just as you didn't choose to have Bob throw you out and replace you with a woman called Mary. You sure know how to pick 'em, Erin,' he shook his head. 'Now eat your breakfast. And no more talking until I've finished eating. I hate arguing with a pretty woman when I'm eating.'

'You——'

'I mean it, Erin,' his eyes were like green chips of glass. 'Eat.'

She did so, reluctantly at first, and then with increasing enjoyment as her appetite returned.

Josh drank several cups of coffee with his meal, the eager Marie always seeming to be on hand to refill his cup, her manner cooler when she served Erin.

'Right,' he finally sat back, his plate completely empty now, a satisfied smile to his lips. He eyed her half-eaten food. 'Is that all you can manage?' he frowned.

She nodded, having sat back in amazement as Josh had eaten all the fried food on his plate, plus the wheatcakes and a couple of rounds of toast. It had taken her all her time to eat what she had, and in truth it hadn't been much.

Josh's frown deepened, his wide brow furrowed. 'Will that get you through the day?'

'Usually,' she nodded again.

He shook his head. 'I think you should see a doctor——'

'Don't be silly,' she gave a dismissive laugh. 'My body has just got used to taking in less, that's all.'

'Have you ever heard of anorexia nervosa?'

'Of course—I haven't got that!' she scorned, having heard a lot in the media about the dieting disease that could kill people if they weren't helped soon enough.

'Maybe not yet,' he conceded. 'But you're headed that way. You need feeding up, three good meals a day.'

'After which I would probably be as big as an elephant,' she smiled. 'I've always had a tendency to put on weight easily.'

'Contrary to popular belief, most men prefer a woman with a little flesh on their bones,' he rasped harshly.

'Show me one,' she laughed.

'You're looking at him.' He gazed steadily back at her as her eyes widened in disbelief.

'You have to be thin nowadays to look good in clothes,' she defended the fashion of being boyishly slender.

'It's no good looking good in clothes if you look awful without them,' he derided.

'I don't look awful——'

'Granted,' Josh nodded. 'From the little I saw when that guy almost had your shirt off I would say you have a nice little body. I just think you should be a little more concerned about the fact that you can no longer eat a normal sized meal.'

Erin was still blushing over the fact that he thought she had a 'nice little body', but unconcerned about her eating problem. That he had noticed her body at all came as something of a surprise to her, that he liked it made her feel selfconscious.

'I'll be fine once I get back to England,' she assured him.

'And when will that be?'

'I—I'm not sure.' She evaded those all-seeing green eyes. 'Next month, maybe,' she lied.

'Why not now? You have nothing to keep you here, do you?'

'I—no. I came over to see my father, but it didn't work out.'

'Tell me about it,' Josh prompted softly.

'There isn't a lot to tell,' she said awkwardly. The pain was still too new for her to talk about it unemotionally.

'Tell me anyway,' Josh insisted.

She told him the bare outline of her visit to her father, aware that he was astute enough to read between the lines, and by the sympathy in his eyes he had done that very well.

When she had finished he just nodded. 'So now you're alone in Calgary?'

'Yes.'

'So why don't you go home?'

'Because I don't have the money! I'm sorry,' she sighed, 'I didn't mean to shout. But it's so expensive living in Calgary. It's going to take me months to get the money together for my return ticket.' Without realising it she contradicted her previous statement about returning next month.

'Not necessarily,' Josh put in softly.

'Oh, it will,' she nodded. 'I wasn't expecting to be returning, so what little savings I did have I spent on a few new clothes. And I'm not getting on very well with my saving here.' She straightened in her chair. 'Which reminds me, I should be going. Thank you for breakfast, Mr Hawke, but I have to go and get myself another job now.'

His hand on her arm stayed her move to stand up. 'What sort of job?'

Erin shrugged. 'The same as I've been doing, I suppose.'

'Cleaning and making beds?'

'Yes,' she answered resentfully. 'There always seem to be those types of jobs going.'

'Oh, there are,' Josh nodded. 'I know of one myself.'

'You do? Where—No, I can't ask you for any more help,' she sighed. 'You've been very kind already. In fact, I should be buying you breakfast.' She pulled the notes out of her pocket that Mike had given her for her wages, giving a rueful laugh. 'I think you must have frightened Mike—he overpaid me!'

'Put it away, Erin,' Josh instructed in a voice that brooked no argument. 'When I invite someone out to eat I don't expect them to pay for it. And I meant it about the job. Are you interested?'

Pride warred with necessity, and finally necessity won. 'Yes, I suppose I am. It would be the same sort of thing, cleaning, stuff like that?'

'Stuff like that,' he nodded. 'What you have to decide is whether or not you would find *my* sexual harassment any more acceptable that you did Mike Johnston's.'

CHAPTER THREE

ERIN swallowed hard, licking her lips as they suddenly seemed too stiff to speak, searching his strong, hard face for some sign of the teasing mockery he seemed to treat her with.

She could see none. Josh was gazing steadily back at her, seemingly waiting for her answer. But what could she answer to a suggestion like that?

'I—What did you say?' she finally asked huskily.

'I think you heard me, Erin,' he drawled, his mouth twisting.

'Yes, but—I don't understand!'

'Then perhaps I'd better explain myself,' he taunted. 'I live alone, and after a winter of cooking and cleaning for myself, of being without female company——'

'Now that I don't believe!' she scorned. This man had a lazy charm that attracted women like bees around honey.

'But it's true. I've been working——'

'Doing what?'

'Time enough for that later,' he dismissed. 'I'd just got to the part where I've denied myself female company,' he derided. 'Meeting you has made me decide it's time to change all that. You're good at cleaning, and anyone can cook. Your references as a lover aren't all that good, but——'

'That's because——'

'You've been choosing the wrong men,' he erroneously finished her outburst. 'You respond beautifully to me.'

'Well, really!' Erin gasped.

'Yes, really,' he mocked in that lazy drawl. 'A few lessons

and you'll be just perfect.'

Erin was very pale, wondering when this nightmare was going to end. 'Lessons you intend giving me, I suppose?' she said hollowly.

'Of course.'

She shook her head. 'Are you insane, Mr Hawke, or am I?'

'Neither of us, honey,' he squeezed the hand he still held. 'And I haven't finished explaining yet. Now I have reason to go to London in a couple of weeks' time——'

'London?' she echoed in a dreamlike voice.

'Yes,' Josh smiled. 'Like to go with me?'

'Go with you?' she squeaked.

'You're beginning to sound like a parrot,' he teased.

'But I—— You said go with you?' she asked eagerly.

'Yes,' he said suddenly serious again. 'In return for your taking care of the house—and me, I'll buy you your ticket back to London. What do you say?'

What did she say? A chance to go back to London in two weeks and not the months she had envisaged. But at what a price!

But why not? Joshua Hawke was a devastatingly attractive man, had already shown himself to be an accomplished lover, so why not accept his offer? At least she would be getting something back for what every other man seemed to want to take for nothing.

But to share a bed with this man, with a complete stranger—was getting back to London worth that?

Josh watched all the different emotions flickering across her face, the consternation, the doubt, the bewilderment. 'Is it yes or no?' he prompted hardly.

'I—I don't know,' she muttered. 'I—It seems a bit—drastic to me.'

Humour quirked his mouth. 'I don't think I've ever heard sharing a bed with me called "drastic" before——'

'There's a first time for everything,' Erin snapped.

'There sure is,' he grinned, underterred by her attitude. 'But it won't be the first time for you, will it?'

Her eyes widened as she took in the implication of his words. If she said yes, would he withdraw his offer? She had a feeling he would. 'No,' she said shakily.

Josh reached into the breast pocket of his denim jacket and took out a piece of paper. 'Do you have a pen?'

'In my bag,' she answered in a puzzled voice, taking one out and handing it to him.

He wrote something down on the piece of paper. 'Here,' he handed it to her, 'take the rest of the day to think over my offer. You can leave a message for me at that telephone number any time until four o'clock. After that I'll have left town.' He picked up his hat, preparing to leave.

Erin put her pen away and picked up the piece of paper. 'I—Where is this?'

'A friend's house, the same friend that's servicing my pick-up for me. He'll be there all day, call him if you want me to pick you up someplace.' He stood up.

Erin looked up at him with wide eyes. 'Where are you going?'

'I have some business in town.'

'You never did tell me what work you do,' she frowned.

'Time enough for that if you decide to take me up on my offer, and if you don't . . . Well, then it won't matter.' He picked up the bill, tipping his hat to her. 'See ya.'

Erin watched in frustrated silence as he moved to the desk to pay for their meal, the infatuated Marie moving hastily to take his money, giggling and blushing as he talked softly to her.

Damn him! He had just propositioned her, and now he was walking out of her life as if she meant nothing to him.

Maybe she didn't, except as someone to cook and clean for him—and share his bed. Two weeks of having a man like that for a lover could leave her more scarred than she was already.

But London! It beckoned like a pair of warm arms on a cold day. She liked Canada, but for all she had been born here she felt alien, longed for the rush and bustle of England's capital, for the sight of the familiar black taxis, a red bus, the pigeons in Trafalgar Square. No matter where she had been born, London was her home, and she longed for it with a desperation that bordered on panic.

Enough to become Joshua Hawke's lover? She baulked at the word *mistress*, the description sounded subservient. It would simply be a job, like any other, with no emotion involved, and a plane ticket back to London would be her wages.

But for a girl who had only ever had three boy-friends in her life, and only one of them during the last year, it seemed a big step to take. Too big a step? That was what she had to decide.

Marie gave her another curious look as she left, her suitcase in one hand, her bag slung over the other shoulder. Erin's head went high. If she accepted Josh's offer she would have to get used to such looks.

And she was seriously considering it. Maybe it was time she got something back from men. Admittedly she would be giving him something in return, but if she had to lose her virginity, and it seemed she would one of these days, perhaps unwillingly, then she would rather it be with Joshua Hawke. He had shown her tenderness and passion in the few brief minutes she had spent in his arms, and surely that was better than any false declaration of love?

She spent most of the day trudging around Calgary, but she knew in her heart she had already decided what she was going to do. And she wasn't even shocked by her decision. She had taken so many knocks lately, a couple of them serious ones, that her emotions felt numb, a dull acceptance of her fate was in her deep blue eyes. She should be flattered, she thought hysterically, she was to share Josh's bed after a winter of abstinence, and from the way Marie had flirted with him many other women would gladly take her place. ·

The telephone was answered after three or four rings, the number recited back to her in a light male voice.

Which didn't help her one little bit. 'Er—who is that?' she asked huskily.

'Dave,' he supplied cheerfully. 'And you have to be Erin,' his tone was warm. 'Josh told me to expect your call.'

Oh, he had, had he! 'I—How did you know it was Erin?' she frowned her puzzlement.

'Josh—mentioned that you were English.'

He probably hadn't mentioned it at all, he seemed to find her English accent very amusing, and no doubt he had passed his amusement on to his friend. 'I believe I can leave a message with you?' she said stiltedly.

'Plans have changed, Erin,' Dave cut in in that cheerful voice. 'He may be delayed, so he wants you to meet him here.'

She drew in an angry breath, having the feeling that Joshua Hawke was taking over her life. And wasn't she giving him that right, didn't she welcome it even, tired of being alone, of having to look after herself in a world that suddenly seemed to have turned alien? She had taken so much this last year—her mother's death, Bob's betrayal, her father's rejection, Mike's brutality, that she felt relieved to give herself into Joshua Hawke's care. And he would ultimately take her back to London, where she would never have to see him again, could forget the way she had sold herself to him.

'You still there, Erin?' Dave asked anxiously.

'Yes,' she confirmed huskily.

'I thought you'd rung off for a moment,' he answered in a relieved voice. 'Josh wouldn't have liked that.'

Wouldn't he, indeed! 'Where exactly is "here"?' she changed the subject.

'Stupid of me,' he laughed, giving her instructions how to get to his home.

'Thank you, Mr——'

'Dave,' he insisted. 'Any friend of Josh's is a friend of mine. I'll see you later, Erin.'

She didn't go straight to Dave's house, having an hour or two to kill before it reached the four o'clock Josh had originally said he intended leaving. Instead she went and got a cup of coffee, lingering over it.

What would Josh have told his friend about her? How would he have explained away the fact that she had a suitcase with her and obviously intended staying with him? Maybe he wouldn't have made any explanations; he didn't look the sort of man who felt he had to explain himself to anyone.

Dave's first words seemed to contradict this. 'Boy, I wish I could join you and Josh—although I doubt you'd welcome an unwanted third,' he added ruefully. 'But I just hate being in town this time of year. With Stampede coming up the city is just filling up with tourists. Whoops— you aren't one, are you?'

'No,' Erin laughed, liking this man immediately, liking his friendliness, his boyishly blond good looks. He was aged about thirty, and unlike Josh, he didn't look it. He was short, with a slender build, wearing the inevitable denims and tee-shirt, the latter covered in grease where he had been working on Josh's pick-up, the brown dusty vehicle parked outside the house. His blond hair was brushed back from his face from a centre parting, almost shoulder-length, his eyes a deep, laughing blue. 'But I'd like to see the Stampede,' she added shyly.

'Your first summer here?' Dave sat down in the chair opposite her, uncaring of his grease-covered clothes.

Erin smiled at the movement. Dave had just proved beyond doubt that he wasn't married—no husband would dare to sit on this lovely furniture in such dirty clothes! Dave's bachelor state surprised her, for the house seemed to have been decorated with a woman in mind. Maybe he was divorced? Erin was realist enough to know that it happened all too often these days, although she hoped that when she finally took that step that she would have the courage to settle any problems she and her husband might have. It was strangely ironic to be thinking of marriage when she was calmly moving in with Joshua Hawke, knowing there was no question of a future for them.

'Yes, my first summer,' she confirmed softly, confused by her thoughts.

Dave nodded. 'Then you definitely have to see Stampede. Ask Josh to take you.'

She knew she wouldn't do any such thing! 'Maybe,' she said noncommittally. 'When is it?'

He gave a disbelieving laugh. 'How long did you say you've been in Calgary?'

'I didn't,' she smiled. 'But I think it's been a couple of months now.'

'And you don't know when Stampede is? Shame on you!'

She laughed at his teasing manner. 'Sorry. I haven't had a lot of time——'

'You can't have done,' he shook his head. 'Two more weeks and this city will be in uproar. There'll be a parade down the city centre——'

'*This* city centre?' She couldn't imagine the busy streets of Calgary without their constant stream of traffic.

'Unbelievable, isn't it?' Dave nodded. 'But they do it

somehow. Then the next day Stampede starts in earnest. There's the rodeo——'

'With real steer-roping and bucking broncos?' Her eyes were wide.

'Real ones,' Dave laughingly confirmed. 'And in the evening there's the chuckwagon racing.'

'Those huge old wagons in races?' Erin gasped, sure they must be too cumbersome.

'Not quite.' His mouth twisted. 'They've been modified for speed. But it's still exciting. And there's exhibitions, livestock, a huge funfair with sideshows. You name it, they've got it!'

She hadn't been to a funfair since she was a child, and her expression was unknowingly wistful.

'I'm sure Josh will take you,' Dave said gently. 'He usually goes once during the ten days.'

'We're going to England in two weeks.'

'I know. But you'll have time before you leave. Hey, I'm a bad host, would you like a coffee or anything? Or how about lemonade?' he added as she was about to refuse. 'The real stuff,' he added temptingly, 'not the manufactured kind.'

'Well . . . okay,' she accepted. 'Thank you.'

He was back from the kitchen seconds later, a brimming glassful of pink lemonade in his hand. 'I'd better go shower and shave. All right if I leave you for a while?'

'Of course,' she assured him hastily, having been dreading personal questions about herself and Josh. 'I'll be fine.'

He nodded. 'I shouldn't be long.'

'Don't rush on my account.' She sipped her lemonade appreciatively.

It was good to be able to relax for a few minutes, her body tensed for Josh's arrival. She suddenly felt embarrassed about meeting him again, her presence here being an indication of her willingness to share his bed.

She stood up restlessly, moving agitatedly about the room. A photograph on top of the stereo caught and held her attention. It was a photograph of Dave and a pretty dark-haired girl, the two of them looking lovingly into each other's eyes.

Erin looked up with a start as Dave came back into the room, wearing a clean pair of denims and a checked shirt, his hair still damp from his shower. His expression darkened as he saw the photograph in her hand.

Erin replaced it at once. 'I—I'm sorry. I—She's very beautiful,' she said lamely.

'Yes,' Dave agreed abruptly, 'she was.'

'Was?' Her eyes widened with bewilderment.

'She died.' He turned away, all boyishness erased as he looked older than his thirty years. 'Josh is late,' he murmured, looking at his wrist-watch, the time already after five.

God, she was an idiot! She had obviously reopened a wound that hadn't even healed the first time around; Dave's eyes were darkly shadowed.

'Would you rather I waited outside?' she asked softly.

'Hell, no!' He seemed to shed his despondency with effort, his smile not quite as natural as it had been before his shower. 'I guess I'm still a little sensitive where Sharon's concerned. It happened just over a year ago, and I'm still not over it.'

'I understand,' Erin sympathised. 'My mother died a year ago too, and I still miss her.' Especially this last few weeks.

'That's rough,' he shook his head.

'Not as rough as losing your wife——'

'We weren't married,' he cut in harshly. 'Sharon died a month before the wedding. You thought we were married because of the house, didn't you?'

'Well . . . yes.'

'We furnished and decorated it together,' he revealed huskily. 'I haven't changed a thing.'

'It's all—perfect.' And it was. Everywhere was golds and browns, the furniture elegant but comfortable.

Dave nodded. 'Sharon had a flair for things like that. She was very artistic.'

'I didn't mean to upset you,' Erin sighed her regret.

'You haven't,' he smiled. 'It's good to talk about her. I don't know why it is, but everyone seems to assume that because someone you loved died they cease to have ever existed. I can't remember the last time anyone mentioned Sharon.'

'Perhaps they're trying to spare you pain,' she pointed out gently.

'I'd rather talk about her than bottle all my memories of her up inside me.'

'I know.'

'Of course you do. Your mother—you were close to her?'

'Yes.'

'Then you do know how I feel. I——' he broke off. 'I think I heard Josh.'

Erin instantly stiffened, the tension back. 'You—you do?'

'Yep,' his easy-going grin was back, the shadows going from his eyes, 'I'd know that walk anywhere.'

She listened. 'I can't hear a thing,' she shook her head.

'You will,' he said with certainty. 'It's Josh all right.' There was the sound of the door opening and shutting, and a few seconds later Joshua Hawke entered the room.

Erin's breath caught in her throat as she looked at him. She had pushed to the back of her mind the raw masculinity of him, the sensuality that oozed out of every pore of his body, his green-eyed gaze seeming to strip the clothes from her body before he turned to look at Dave, his eyes narrowing as he took in the other man's damp hair.

What on earth was he thinking? Did he really think that just because she had spent an hour or so alone with Dave she had automatically been to bed with him? Two spots of angry colour heightened her cheeks.

Josh turned back to her. 'You got here okay, then.'

'Obviously,' she said tautly.

'Like a beer, Josh?' Dave cut through the tension, seemingly unaware of it—or else very tactful.

'Thanks,' the other man accepted tersely, not taking his eyes off Erin.

'More lemonade, Erin?' Dave smiled at her.

'No, thanks, I've had enough.' She deliberately infused warmth into her voice, ignoring Josh as she smiled at Dave.

'I won't be long.' Dave left the two of them alone together, the twitching of his lips seeming to tell her that he knew exactly what was going on.

Josh moved with long strides to sit beside her on the sofa, putting his hat on the floor beside him, his arm falling casually across her shoulders. 'So, what did you do with your day?' His tone was friendly now, his closeness unnerving.

But Erin refused to be unnerved, shrugging out of the arc of his arm to sit away from him. 'I didn't spend any of it in Dave's bed, if that's what you want to know!' she snapped, glaring at him.

Josh smiled infuriatingly. 'I know that,' he drawled.

'I don't see how——'

'I know, Erin,' he repeated firmly, moving along the sofa to sit close to her again, his face only inches away from hers. 'I'm still waiting for my hello kiss,' he said softly.

'Then you can go on waiting!' she snapped. 'I——' her

protest was cut off by his mouth being placed firmly over hers.

It was a kiss he intended taking full pleasure from, parting her lips with the tip of his tongue, the kiss deepening, taking on new dimensions as her mouth parted to accept the intimacy of his.

To a girl crying out for affection it was impossible to resist the pull of this kiss; she was unable to stop the involuntary movement of her arms going up about his throat, her hands tangled in the hair at his nape, loving its silky texture, the way her movements seemed to entice Josh on to further intimacies.

Josh's eyes smiled into hers as he slowly pulled her back to him. 'Enjoy it, Erin. I am.'

'But Dave——'

'Enjoy!' he murmured against her lips, his kiss slow and drugging.

Erin looked at him dazedly when he at last raised his head, much more shaken than he appeared to be, his eyes deeply amused.

'Lesson number one,' he smiled.

'How did I do?' She saw his eyes widen, as if he was surprised by her calmness. No doubt he had expected her to lose her temper at his mockery, but she was past that. This afternoon she had decided to accept her fate, and she would keep to that decision.

'B-plus,' Josh drawled, sitting back from her, his arm now resting along the sofa.

Erin fluttered her eyelashes at him. 'Only B-plus?'

'You would have got an A-minus if you hadn't pulled back when I——'

'When you kissed me,' she finished blushingly knowing exactly what he had been going to say. But she had never been kissed with such intimacy, and for a few moments it had surprised her.

'Mm,' he grinned. 'And don't flutter your eyelashes at me again,' he told her sternly. 'Some men might like it, but I don't.'

'Sorry!' her sarcasm was unmistakable. 'I thought that was the way I was supposed to act.'

His face darkened ominously. 'Let's get one thing clear, Erin. You chose to meet me here, and by doing so you accepted our relationship. If you've changed your mind, fine, I'm not making you stay. But don't try to act the whore to make me feel guilty——'

'Oh, I didn't——'

'Yes, you did. And it won't work. No one is forcing you to do anything. Are they?' he insisted hardly.

'No,' Erin sighed. 'I'm sorry—I'll behave.'

'I'm on my way in!' Dave shouted before entering the room, two bottles of beer in his hands.

'It took you long enough,' Josh grinned as the other man almost threw the bottle at him. 'Thanks,' and he took a long swig from the opened bottle.

'Okay, buddy,' Dave nodded, drinking his own beer. 'As for the time it took, I had to wait until it was safe to come in. After all, Erin is a beautiful woman.'

'She certainly is,' Josh drawled, his gaze moving appreciatively over her flushed face. 'Almost ready to leave, honey?'

She suffered the endearment without protest. 'Whenever you are,' she nodded.

He finished his beer in one swallow, wiping his mouth with the back of his hand before standing up. 'Thanks for doing the truck, Dave. I appreciate it. I owe you one.'

'Forget it,' the other man dismissed. 'Bring the car over some time, I'd be glad to check it over.'

'I'll bet,' Josh grinned, putting out a hand to pull Erin to her feet. 'I'll think about it.'

'Will I see you again before you go to England?'

Josh frowned. 'Maybe, maybe not. Depends if I get the time.'

'Erin would like to go to Stampede,' Dave smiled conspiratorially at her.

Deep green eyes levelled on her, her hand still firmly held in his. 'Would you?' Josh asked.

'Well . . .'

'Everyone should go to the Calgary Stampede once in their life,' Dave encouraged.

'I'll take you,' Josh told Erin huskily.

'You don't have to.' She was embarrassed about Dave mentioning it. Josh might not want to take her out, to possibly be seen with her by other of his friends.

'I said I'll take you.' He raised his eyes heavenwards at Dave. 'You give a woman what she wants and then she says she doesn't want it! I'll never understand them!'

'And you're such a novice,' his friend mocked.

'Oh, I know he isn't that, Dave,' Erin said confidently. 'Otherwise I wouldn't be here.' She looked at Josh defiantly. If he could taunt her in front of the other man then she could do the same. She might have agreed to go with him, but that didn't mean he had the right to mock her any time he felt like it.

His hand moved to caress her throat, the light of revenge in his eyes. 'So sharp-tongued now, but you didn't feel that way this morning in my bed.'

Erin gasped, first blushing, and then paling. She should have known he would get back at her two-fold! He had already shown her that he was by far the quicker-witted of the two of them—would she ever learn?

She couldn't even look at Dave as they said their goodbyes; she was too embarrassed. She struggled to get into the pick-up, surprised at how high it was off the ground.

'Need a leg up?' Josh taunted.

'Certainly not!' she flashed, climbing agilely up into the cab. It seemed even higher once she was sitting inside, towering over the cars travelling down the road.

Josh swung in beside her, grinning down at Dave. 'She's an independent little miss.'

'I gathered,' the other man laughed. 'Good luck in England.'

'Thanks,' Josh accepted, serious now, as he started the pick-up and moved out into the traffic.

Erin stared woodenly in front of her. 'I would say independent is the last thing I'm being by going with you.'

'Don't be bitter,' he said lightly.

'I'm not bitter,' she sighed, turning to look at him, easily sitting three feet away from him on the length of the seat. 'But I wish you hadn't told Dave—implied that——'

'Just staking ownership, Erin,' he drawled.

'Ownership——!'

'What else would you call it?' He quirked one black eyebrow beneath the rim of his hat, his eyes narrowed against the sun.

He looked like a marauding cowboy, rugged and virile, his face weathered and lined beyond his thirty-four years, and in a way it was flattering to think such a handsome man had chosen her, Erin Richards, to share his life, his bed, for two weeks. Better than a false offer of a lifetime! she thought bitterly.

'It's as good a description as any, I suppose,' she shrugged.

Josh chuckled. 'Complacency I never expected.'

'Complacency you aren't getting,' her eyes flashed. 'Don't worry, I'll make sure you enjoy it,' she snapped.

His face tautened, the skin stretching tightly over his high cheekbones. 'Not if I bed a shrew,' he rasped.

Erin shook her head mockingly. 'You don't want complacency, and now you don't want reaction either——'

'Oh, I want reaction, but not the verbal kind.'

Colour flooded her cheeks, and she turned to look out of the window. They were leaving town, heading west towards the mountains on Highway 1. The Canadian Rockies looked regal in the evening sunshine, some of them still snow-capped. It was soothing to look at such timeless beauty, and Erin felt some of the tension leaving her.

'Where exactly do you live?' she asked interestedly after several minutes of silent awe; the mountainous peaks seemed to go on for ever. But surely there weren't any other towns out here? She remembered looking on the map before coming to Canada, and the nearest town in this direction was Banff. Did Josh live there?

'About twenty miles from town,' he instantly shot the idea down.

She frowned. 'Twenty miles . . .? But if you live that close why did you stay at the motel last night?' Last night? Was it only last night? It seemed much longer, so much had happened in that short time.

He overtook a cruising car with ease. 'You forget, Dave was servicing the pick-up. Besides, after a night on the town, a deserved one I might add, I was over the limit for driving.'

'I—Mind the little animal!' she cried, clutching at Josh's arm as a little animal like an English grey squirrel stood in the middle of the road in front of them, making no move to avoid their death-giving wheels.

Josh shook off her hand, swerving, easily missing the little furry creature. 'Don't ever grab my arm like that again when I'm driving!' he ground out, shooting her a furious look from angry green eyes.

'I—Sorry.' Erin turned in her seat to see if the tiny creature had moved, seeing it running to the side of the road, breathing her relief as she turned back to Josh. 'What was it?'

'Richardson's ground squirrel,' he said tersely, obviously still angry with her.

'Oh, how cute!'

'Very,' he agreed dryly. 'Unless you happen to be a rancher.'

'Oh?' she asked interestedly, sensing his anger was lessening.

'Being ground squirrels they live in the ground,' he explained patiently.

'Well, obviously,' Erin said crossly. 'Don't be patronising!'

'Sorry,' he smiled. 'But the holes those "cute" little creatures dig as burrows can do a lot of damage to a horse or cow.'

'Of course. What a shame! They—they don't shoot them, do they?' she looked at him with wide eyes.

'Some of them do,' Josh confirmed callously. 'Some poison them.'

'How cruel!'

His mouth twisted. 'And that from a girl who lived in a country where they send about twenty hounds out after one little fox, and sit and watch as they rip it to shreds.'

Erin shuddered. 'I don't approve of foxhunting either.'

Josh shrugged. 'It may be cruel to kill those squirrels, but it's even crueller if your livestock breaks a leg in one of their holes. It could be in agony for hours before you discovered its fate.'

Erin looked at him closely. 'You sound as if you speak from experience.'

'I do. And believe me, it isn't pretty.'

'No, I—Oh look, there's another one!'

'Calm down,' Josh sighed, again avoiding the small animal. 'You almost give me a heart attack every time you shout like that.'

'Sorry,' she gave a rueful smile. 'But why do they come

out on to the road like that? They could get killed.'

'They often do. It's the heat of the road that attracts them. It's dark and retains the heat of the sun, and they like that. And if one of them happens to get killed . . . his little friends will come along and eat him!' Josh told her with relish, laughing at her shocked expression.

'Ugh!' she groaned, pulling a face.

Josh grinned at her. 'Still think they're cute?'

She gave him an angry frown. 'I don't believe you, you're just saying that to shock me.'

He shook his head. 'They eat mainly vegetation, but if a little dead meat comes their way they aren't going to complain.'

She grimaced. 'They really eat *each other*?'

'Sure.'

'That's disgusting!'

'That's survival,' he corrected.

'It somehow doesn't seem right that they should live off each other in that way.'

'I don't see why—human beings do it all the time,' he said dryly.

Erin paled. 'That—that was cruel!' she choked.

He gave a puzzled frown, glancing at her. 'What the hell——? I didn't mean you, for God's sake! Don't be so damned sensitive,' he scowled. 'You won't be living off me, you'll be working *for* me.'

'If you say so,' she said moodily, staring out of the window.

Josh raised one eyebrow. 'You don't believe me?'

'I suppose it could be called work——'

'Let's forget that aspect of it for the moment,' he sighed. 'For some reason it seems to upset you.'

Forget it? How could she forget it? As the time neared evening sharing Josh's bed became more and more of a reality—and it terrified her, not upset her! She must have been mad to agree to this, mad!

'Maybe this will help cheer you up.' Josh reached into
the breast pocket of his denim jacket and handed her an
envelope. 'Look inside,' he invited.

'Inside . . .?'

'Go ahead,' he nodded.

She couldn't imagine what could be inside the envelope
that would 'cheer her up'. When she saw the airline folder
inside she knew, as she took out two Air Canada tickets,
from Calgary to London.

'To show you that I mean to keep my side of the bar-
gain,' he drawled.

Erin pushed the tickets back into the envelope, thrusting
them at him. 'Then you'd better hang on to these until
I've kept my side.'

'Maybe,' he agreed grimly, anger flaring in his eyes as
he put the envelope back in his pocket.

She stared moodily out of the side window for several
minutes, blind to the change in their surroundings; the
flat, almost treeless countryside was now giving way to a
hillier terrain, dark green pine trees starting to edge the
road in parts, the mountains coming even closer.

She licked her lips, forcing the words out. 'Your friend
Dave, does he know—Did you tell him——'

'About our deal?' Josh finished dryly. 'Did you think I
might?'

'How should I know?' she snapped. 'The two of you
seem—close.'

'We are. But my private life remains just that, private.
Why, wouldn't you have liked him to know?' His eyes
were narrowed.

'Well, I—Surely it's just between the two of us?'

He nodded. 'I think so. Did you like Dave?'

She shrugged. 'He seemed very nice, but sort of sad.'

'Sad?' Josh echoed sharply. 'Why do you say that?'

'Because of his girl-friend. It must have been awful for him.'

Josh was very tense, a white line of tension about his mouth. 'Dave told you about Sharon?'

Erin swallowed hard. What had she said? Josh was suddenly furiously angry, and it seemed to be because she had mentioned Dave's girl-friend.

'Shouldn't he have done?' she asked nervously.

'It depends what he told you,' he said tautly.

'Just that she died a month before their wedding,' Erin frowned.

'Sharon didn't die,' he told her harshly. 'She committed suicide.'

Erin gulped. 'She—she what?'

'She killed herself!' Josh rasped.

'I—That's terrible!' Erin gasped, unable to believe that beautiful girl had taken her own life.

'It's worse than terrible. She was beautiful, Erin, both inside and out. And I still miss her like hell.'

'You—you miss her?' her eyes were wide.

'Shouldn't I?' he said bitterly.

It seemed that he should. Had Dave known that Josh, his best friend, also loved Sharon? No wonder Josh had reacted so violently when she had scorned his concern that *she* might commit suicide!

CHAPTER FOUR

THEY drove on in silence, Erin shocked by what Josh had just told her. She was so deep in thought she didn't even notice that they had turned off the highway and were now driving down a narrow road into thick pine trees. But she did notice when they took a right-hand turn on to what amounted to nothing more than a gravel dirt-track, the suspension on the pick-up such that she bounced across the seat, almost landing up on the floor, such had been her relaxed state.

Josh burst out laughing at the spectacle she made sprawled out on the seat next to him.

'Very funny,' she scowled, as she picked herself up, brushing dust off her denims.

He still smiled. 'Maybe I should have warned you about that.'

Erin gave him a look of disgust, looking around her as they seemed to be going deeper into the trees, tall pines towering either side of the narrow dirt-track. 'Where on earth are we?' she demanded to know.

'On our way to my home,' he answered infuriatingly.

'I know that!' she sighed. 'But *where* are we?'

He laughed softly. 'Not in the wilderness, I can assure you.'

Erin's apprehension deepened. 'You didn't tell me you lived all the way out here!' There was just nothing here except trees, and presumably Josh's home!

'Does it make any difference?' he mocked.

'I—No, I suppose not,' but her voice lacked conviction.

'Don't worry,' he taunted softly, 'I'll help you with the

more menial tasks, like chopping wood and carrying in the water.'

'Chopping wood . . .? And carrying in water? From a river or a well?' she squeaked.

'A well.'

She looked at him closely, sure that he must be teasing her. 'You really have a well?'

'I really do,' he confirmed with a sincerity that couldn't be doubted.

'God!' she breathed. 'But surely you won't need logs this time of year?' After all, it was June!

'It can get cold at night out here without central heating,' he shrugged. 'Even in summer. Besides, now is the time to stock up for winter.'

'You're coming back here for winter?' Her eyes widened.

'It's the best time of year,' Josh nodded. 'Fewer people in town, and plenty of snow for skiing. Do you ski?'

'No,' she laughed. 'There isn't a lot of opportunity for it in South London.'

'Someone should teach you, you would enjoy it.'

Once again Erin frowned. 'Aren't the conditions out here a little—primitive?' She hesitated over the word, but really there was no other description for the life he was mapping out for her.

'I suppose so,' he accepted. 'But I like it. Especially now that you'll be doing most of the work,' he added happily.

Her heart sank. She had envisaged doing his cooking and washing, keeping the house clean, but she hadn't imagined it would be so lacking in modern conveniences.

A sudden thought struck her. 'Do you have a washing machine?'

Josh shook his head, much to her dismay. 'No electricity.'

'No elec . . .?' She gulped. That meant no lighting, no

dishwasher, and worst of all, no stove. 'How do you cook?'

'I have an old range,' he said cheerfully. 'Another reason we need the logs.'

This was getting worse! These were things she should have found out before agreeing to come with him. She wasn't equipped to manage under these conditions. And after all the work he was expecting her to do how did he expect her to have enough energy to share his bed at night?

She gave Josh a suspicious look, sure that he must be teasing her. He met her gaze with steady green eyes, raising an eyebrow questioningly.

'Nothing,' she muttered, wondering just what she had let herself in for the next two weeks. At the time Josh had made the offer she had thought he was overpaying her, now she wasn't so sure.

Suddenly there was a clearing in the trees, revealing a huge farmhouse and the accompanying stables and barns that went to make up a small ranch. Horses grazed in the meadow, so many Erin couldn't count them.

She turned hopefully to Josh. 'Is this . . .?'

'Nope,' he laughed, bringing the pick-up to a halt in front of the house. 'Some friends of mine live here.' He swung easily to the ground. 'Come on,' he invited before slamming the door.

Erin got reluctantly to the ground, going round to the other side of the vehicle to join Josh. 'Are you sure you wouldn't rather I waited here?'

He shook his head. 'You'll like Jim and Martha. Martha will be in the house—come on.' He took hold of her arm, giving a brief knock on the door before entering the house.

Erin hung back. 'What if——'

'Josh!'

Erin looked up in time to see a young blonde-haired woman launching herself into Josh's waiting arms, kissing him warmly, a gesture Josh seemed only too happy to return, his arm still about the other woman's shoulders as he turned to face Erin.

Martha looked to be in her mid-twenties, gaminely pretty rather than beautiful, her blonde wavy hair medium length, her figure slender in denim shorts and a light blue sun-top held up solely by her uptilted breasts, her skin tanned a deep, golden brown.

'Martha, this is Erin Richards. Erin, Martha Halliday,' Josh introduced, smiling and relaxed. 'Martha is my cousin.'

'Second cousin,' she laughingly corrected, extending a hand to Erin. 'Pleased to meet you,' she said warmly.

Erin shyly took the proffered hand. 'Thank you.'

'I hope you can both stay to dinner,' Martha invited. 'Jim's going to barbecue a couple of steaks, so there's plenty of food.'

' 'Fraid not,' Josh refused. 'Where is Jim?'

'He thought Sabre seemed a little lame, so he's just gone out to check on him. Sheba's with him, so she probably didn't hear you arrive.'

Erin had no idea who Sabre or Sheba were, all that she was aware of was that Josh had refused dinner for them both. It would have been nice to have left getting to know the range until tomorrow. She couldn't understand why Josh chose to live so primitively, when Martha Halliday obviously had electricity and running water. In fact this house was very luxurious, both inside and out. Although she couldn't honestly say she had seen a house in Canada that she didn't like, they were so much nicer than the lookalike boxes they seemed to build in England.

Josh nodded. 'Are they in the top field?'

'Mm,' Martha nodded. 'Jim's going to bring Sabre down to the stable. He shouldn't be long.'

'I'll go and meet him. You'll be okay, Erin?'

'Fine,' she nodded. It would be childish to say otherwise, although she felt rather shy with the other woman.

'Good girl!' He moved to kiss her lightly on the lips— much to her embarrassment, and the house suddenly seemed quiet as he strode outside into the evening sunshine.

Erin didn't know where to look, aware of Martha's speculative glance. Josh wasn't the type of man to make explanations to anyone for his actions, but he had left her feeling as if she should. 'Josh and I——'

'Like each other,' Martha finished gently. 'You don't have to tell me anything, Erin. It's enough that you're here with Josh. Would you like some coffee?'

'Yes, please,' she sighed her relief of Martha's easy acceptance of her, liking the other woman immensely. So far she had liked all Josh's friends, she just felt uncomfortable with the man himself.

She chatted easily with Martha while they waited for the return of the two men, telling the eager Martha all about England.

'I've always wanted to go there,' the other woman said dreamily. 'Alberta's beautiful, and I never want to move away from here, but we're such a new country. Do you know Alberta only celebrated its seventy-fifth birthday in 1980? England has so much history.'

Erin laughed lightly. 'I hate to tell you this, but most of that history is crumbling into the dust.'

'No, don't spoil it,' Martha laughed. 'I've almost persuaded Jim to take me next year—if I can get him away from his precious horses,' she added ruefully. 'We breed Arabians, and Jim doesn't think anyone else can take care of his horses like he can. A month away from them seems like a crime to him.'

'They look beautiful horses,' and they did, although Erin knew next to nothing about them—except that she didn't like them within six feet of her! Which probably amounted almost to a sin in a country where most people knew how to ride, even if they didn't own, a horse.

Martha nodded. 'We make a living.'

'Is that what Josh does too?' she asked casually.

'Josh?' Martha looked startled. 'But Josh is——' she broke off as the two men could be heard entering the house. 'Excuse me,' she stood up to go and greet them.

Damn! Erin's curiosity about Josh's profession had been about to be answered. It hadn't bothered her at first, but Josh's reluctance to supply any answers himself had made her eager to know. He looked like a rancher or farmer, he even acted like one, she had to admit that, but there was the puzzle of his hands, strong hands, long and sensitive, with not a callous on them. She had put her fate into the hands of an enigma!

Martha came back into the room her hand resting in the crook of the arm of a man with reddish-brown hair and twinkling blue eyes, their complete rapport showing them to be husband and wife. Josh followed them, looking searchingly at Erin, giving her the impression that he knew of her effort to find out more about him.

'Missed me, honey?' he mocked, his arm settling lightly across her shoulders as he joined her on the sofa.

'Should I have done?' she returned coolly, determined this wasn't going to be a repeat of her embarrassment in front of Dave.

The man who had to be Jim Halliday burst out laughing. 'I think I like you already Erin Richards,' he chuckled. 'It isn't often I get to see Josh put in his place. It's good to at last meet the woman who can do it,' and his hand met hers in a strong grasp of welcome.

'I'm more interested in putting Erin in her place,' Josh drawled tauntingly.

She blushed fiery red, knowing exactly where he thought

her 'place' to be. And later on tonight she would be there! She couldn't even get used to the casual way he kissed or touched her whenever he felt like it, staking claim to that ownership he felt was his, let alone imagine letting him make love to her.

He stood up. 'We have to be on our way.' He pulled her effortlessly to her feet, muscles rippling beneath his denim jacket.

'You'll bring Erin back again before you leave?' Martha requested. 'It's so nice to have another woman to talk to for a change instead of you strong, muscular types.'

'Thanks!' her husband said dryly. 'Come over Saturday, Josh?'

'We'll see,' his answer was noncommittal. 'You know me, I never like to make definite plans.'

'Give yourself a break, Josh,' Martha encouraged.

'We'll see,' he tapped her lightly on the nose. 'Don't push, little cousin.'

'You always were infuriating,' she said crossly. 'When you get to the screaming stage, Erin, just make him bring you right over.'

'I'll try,' Erin promised, wondering how many other women had got to the 'screaming stage' while staying with Josh. How many other women had he had living with him?

'Right, let's go,' and Josh more or less pushed her out of the house to the truck.

'Don't do—Oh, my God!' She hastily backed out of the cab of the pick-up, backing farther away as a huge dog launched itself at her. Erin dodged behind Josh, her hands on his shoulders as she peered around his body at the large black dog now licking his hand. 'What is it?' she shuddered.

Josh laughed, pulling her out from behind him. 'Meet Sheba.' He stood her in front of the dog, its huge jaws and lolling pink tongue looking vicious to her.

'I—Where did she come from?' She pressed herself back against him as the dog began to sniff interestedly at her legs, uncaring of the fact that Josh was enjoying the experience immensely.

'Martha and Jim have been looking after her for me while I was away,' he murmured close against her ear.

Erin swallowed hard. 'You mean she's yours?' She turned to look at him, instantly wishing she hadn't as the movement brought his face within inches of her own.

'Yes,' he confirmed softly. 'What's the matter, don't you like dogs?'

She looked down as the dog began to nuzzle against her hand, expecting the huge jaws to close about her flesh at any moment. 'I thought I did,' she muttered nervously.

'Don't tell me,' he mocked. 'There wasn't a lot of opportunity for dogs in South London.'

'Not in a flat there wasn't!' Her eyes flashed at him, aware of the other couple looking on in amusement. 'And stop laughing at me!' she hissed at Josh.

He sighed, putting her away from him. 'Then stop being ridiculous. I would hardly have let you meet Sheba like that if she was in the least vicious.' He moved forward to the dog, bending down to stroke her silky throat. 'Good girl, Sheba,' he murmured affectionately. 'Good girl! Come and say hello.' He took the dog's two front paws and placed them on Erin's shoulders.

Erin looked down horror-struck as the long nose came to rest on her shoulder too.

'She's saying hello,' Josh told her.

'Really?' she squeaked.

'Yes, really.' He gave her an impatient look before putting the dog back down on all fours. 'You'll get used to her.'

Which was fine for him to say, Erin fumed as they drove

on to his home. *He* wasn't the one who was frightened of the lolling beast that sat between them, one eye seeming to be permanently focused on her as Sheba tried to give the impression of being asleep.

'She can sense your fear,' Josh rapped out as she sat stiffly on her side of the seat, as far away from Sheba as she could get.

'I can't help that,' she snapped. 'You should have told me—warned me——'

'Yes,' he agreed heavily. 'But how was I to know you'd be frightened of a little dog?'

'Little? She's *huge*!'

'German Shepherd and Labrador cross-bred,' he said proudly. 'The best cross-breed you can get as far as I'm concerned.'

'Well, of course you would think that,' Erin said agitatedly. 'Although I must say Labradors are lovely dogs,' she added grudgingly.

'Sheba is as gentle as a lamb.' He caressed the dog behind her floppy ears.

Erin snorted disgustedly. 'Lambs don't have teeth like that.'

'I don't suppose you like horses either?' he derided.

She pulled a face. 'Do you have one of those too?'

'A couple. *Don't* you like them?'

'I—Of course I do,' she lied with bravado.

'You ride?'

His surprise angered her. 'Of course.' Her bravado was slipping somewhat, although Josh looked convinced. 'All the time. We do have horses in England too, you know.'

'I'm sure you do. That's fine, then, you can join me for my early morning ride tomorrow.'

'I—I can?' This seemed to be backfiring against her. But she couldn't have said that they didn't have much opportunity for horses in South London either!

'Sure,' he nodded. 'It will put some colour in your cheeks.'

'I think I'd rather have a lie-in——'

'Good idea,' he grinned. 'I'll join you.'

Colour flooded her cheeks. 'I—Maybe going out for a ride would be nice after all.' For a moment she had forgotten she would be sharing his bed! If they both stayed in bed in the morning it was obvious what would happen.

'I don't mind either way,' he shrugged.

How flattering! 'Are we nearly there?' she asked waspishly; the bumpy track was getting on her nerves now.

'Another mile or so.' He quirked an eyebrow at her. 'In a hurry, are you?'

She flushed at his implication. 'I thought maybe you wanted me to chop a few logs before dinner,' she snapped.

His mouth quirked with horror. 'Not tonight.'

'How kind!' Her sarcasm was obvious.

Sheba raised her head to look at Erin, her brown-eyed gaze steady, her mouth open as she breathed, her tongue lolling over her long teeth. Erin instantly fell silent.

She was starting to feel decidedly hungry now, she only hoped it wouldn't take too long to get this damned range started. Maybe they could just have soup or something——

'Martha's mention of steak has made me feel like one—how about you?' Josh interrupted her thoughts.

'Fine,' she agreed wanly. Heavens, it would be midnight before they ate!

As soon as she saw the house she knew Josh had been making a fool of her. It was a long cedarwood bungalow, very modern in design, with Georgian-style windows; a smooth lawn and pretty flower-beds, trees edged the house on three sides, the fourth containing the corral with the two horses, a huge chestnut-coloured stallion and a quieter-looking dark brown gelding.

It was like coming across an oasis in a desert, or in this case, a dream house in the middle of a forest. It was absolutely beautiful.

'You lied to me!' She turned furiously on Josh as he took out the control to the garage, pressing the button that opened the door before driving smoothly inside.

'Did I?' he asked innocently, climbing out of the truck, Sheba following faithfully at his heels.

Erin got out her own side, too angry to admire the black Porsche that was already parked in the garage. 'You know you did,' she stormed, joining him as he strolled over to the corral.

'How did I do that?' he asked casually, stroking the horses affectionately on the muzzle.

'You deliberately let me believe——'

'What you wanted to believe!' His eyes snapped with anger. 'We aren't backward over here, you know. In fact, we have a hell of a lot more to offer than England.'

'I——'

'You were being damned patronising!' He turned to face her, the heel of one boot resting on the bottom rail of the fence, his elbows on the top rail as he pushed his hat to the back of his head. 'And I wasn't lying about the well,' he nodded behind her.

Erin's eyes widened as she took in the small brick well with the slate roof. It looked a little like an English wishing-well. 'Is it real?' She walked over to take a closer look.

'This part of it is just for show,' Josh joined her. 'But there really is a water supply down there, an underground stream, the water more pure than in any English reservoir.'

She looked up with a weary sigh. 'We aren't in competition. I'm sorry if I sounded patronising earlier. It was just that we hadn't discussed where you lived, and it was a surprise to me when you drove out this way.'

He nodded. 'Apology accepted.' His arm went companionably about her shoulders. 'And I shouldn't have teased you,' his tone lightened. 'Except that you're so easy to tease.' He was openly grinning now.

Erin relaxed as his good humour returned. She would rather have him as a friend than an enemy. 'Tell me more about the well,' she invited huskily. 'Do you really get your water from there?'

'Yep,' he nodded. 'The water is about ninety feet down, cold and clear, and it's pumped over to the house. We're lucky, we get about twenty gallons a minute, if we want it, some acreages only get five or six, and they often go short of water.'

'Is the water treated with anything?' She couldn't imagine people drinking untreated water in England, the disease associated with it from olden times was still too vivid in a lot of peoples minds.

'Ours isn't. Sometimes it has too much iron, and then it's treated, but otherwise you're drinking stream-water. Come on, I'll show you the inside of the house. I think you'll like it.'

Erin was sure she would. Even if it weren't beautiful she would have liked it, simply because it had running water and electricity. After what she had been imagining it was a relief to see the luxurious kitchen area, the stove, fridge, dishwasher, walnut cabinets, and cream and marble effect worktops, the floor carpeted. From the kitchen they entered what in England she would have called a living-room, but over here she knew it was called a family room, the open brick fireplace the centrepiece of the room, the comfortable furniture arranged accordingly.

The fireplace served two rooms, a lounge on the other side of the wall, the dining-room at the end of this, every room having the same gold and brown mottled carpet.

'The bedrooms are through the back,' Josh informed

her as her eyes widened with the luxury of what she had already seen.

Erin stopped at the bottom of the staircase just off the lounge. 'And what's up there?'

'My workroom,' he dismissed.

After the cabin she had been expecting this house came as a shock to her, a pleasant shock. For all his casual appearance this house was the last thing in luxury, the four bedrooms just as nicely furnished, the bathroom for the three smaller ones a deep, dark brown.

But the master bedroom was the most luxurious, the room large in itself, the huge double bed covered with a brown continental quilt, the furniture a rich gold, and adjoining this room was the bathroom. Erin gasped as Josh flicked the door open. She had never seen a sunken bath before, let alone bathed in one, and the round cream bath did look very inviting.

'There's a shower in here if you'd prefer it.' Josh opened glass doors to reveal a shower big enough for two people.

Now why had she thought that? She had never bathed or showered with anyone in her life, and she wasn't about to start now!

She looked at Josh with new eyes. In Calgary he had just seemed like a very attractive man who had offered to help her, for a price. But this house, its luxury, pointed to him being more than that.

She licked her lips nervously. 'It's all—very lovely.'

'Thanks,' he smiled. 'I helped design it. Now, let's see,' he opened several of the drawers in the dressing-table. 'You can put your things in here,' he emptied the contents of two of the drawers into the other two.

'No! I mean, surely that isn't necessary,' Erin forced calm into her voice. 'I won't be here long enough for that. I can leave my things in my suitcase.'

'You can put them in here.' Josh didn't even raise his

voice, his tone was enough to tell her that her arguments would be of no avail. He moved to the fitted wardrobe, pushing his clothes to one end. 'Hang the rest of your stuff in here.'

'Josh——'

'I'll go and get your suitcase from the pick-up,' he cut across her protest, leaving the room with long strides.

She looked around her luxurious cage, studiously avoiding the bed. In other circumstances it would have been fun to stay in a house like this, but as Josh's live-in lover it was going to be sheer hell.

She hadn't thought of the emotional side of this situation when she accepted his offer, had thought it would be like sleeping with a stranger, someone she need feel no guilt with, someone easily forgotten once she was back in England. But she was slowly getting to know Josh, he wasn't the sort of man you could push to the background, too forceful a personality for that, and the more she got to know him the more embarrassing this arrangement was turning out to be.

'What's the matter?' He had entered the bedroom without making a noise, studying her pale face with narrowed eyes.

She swallowed hard, chewing on her bottom lip. 'Josh, I don't think I can——'

'Don't try and back out now,' he scowled, dropping the suitcase. 'I'm not driving back to Calgary, and you aren't staying here with me without sharing my bed.'

'But I don't think I can do it.' She looked at him pleadingly, unaware of how small and defenceless she looked.

'And I can't stay here with you without taking you to bed,' he told her bluntly. 'I want you.'

'But——'

'I *want* you, Erin,' he repeated huskily, moving to stand just in front of her, his hands cupping either side of her face, his thumbtips parting her trembling lips. 'I want you,' he murmured before his dark head bent and his mouth took possession of hers.

She stood passively in his arms. This afternoon she had been too shocked to do anything but respond to the potency of his experienced kisses, but here, where the full force of her commitment had come home to her, she could only remember the other men who had used her in her life, their reasons very different, but the pain going just as deep.

She looked at him with cold eyes when he at last lifted his head. 'Another lesson?' Her voice was chill.

'No.' He thrust her away from him. 'God, no wonder that guy Bob threw you out if you only gave him as much response as you just gave me!'

'Bob?' she looked startled. 'But he——'

'Must have had a hell of a lot more patience with you than I have,' Josh snapped disgustedly, his hands thrust into the back pockets of his denims. 'I don't like these sort of games, Erin. You knew the arrangement when you agreed to come here. It's no good trying to back out now. This is my bedroom, that's my bed, and later on tonight you'll be sharing it with me!' He stormed out of the room, a door slammed several minutes later, and the house was suddenly quiet.

Erin stared after him in numbed disbelief. He thought— he had said—heavens, he thought Bob had been her lover! And why shouldn't he? Had she ever explained to him that Bob was her stepfather? She knew she hadn't. She had been too busy wallowing in self-pity to realise what construction he would put on what she told him.

And now he thought—lord, no wonder he had made this crazy suggestion in the first place. He thought she had already lived with a man for a year, so why should she baulk at a couple of weeks spent with him?

She had been a fool, a stupid idiot. And Josh would have to be told the truth about Bob.

But she couldn't find Josh anywhere, not in the house or outside. Sheba was noticeably absent too, so perhaps the two of them had gone for a walk. Erin left her suitcase in Josh's bedroom, but made no effort to unpack it. After she had spoken to him he might decide to return her to Calgary after all. Sleeping on a bench somewhere suddenly became a frightening reality.

She found the makings of coffee in the kitchen and filled the percolator. If Josh was gone for any length of time she might need this coffee to keep her going. A sandwich would have been nice, but she didn't feel she should just help herself, not in the circumstances.

After two cups of the strong coffee she was starting to get restless, getting up from the breakfast bar in the kitchen to start wandering about the house. Josh might have been angry with her, but he had no right to just go off and leave her like this. Were they close enough to the mountains to have bears wandering around? She didn't think so, but then what did she know?

Where was he? She was becoming increasingly angry at his continued absence, sure he was doing it on purpose to punish her.

Then she heard a noise upstairs, a scraping sound. Josh had said he had his workroom up there. Could it be him, or was it an intruder? She cursed herself for her vivid imaginings. Of course it was Josh, but what was he doing up there? Working, obviously. But at what? After the way he had left her she didn't think he would welcome her curiosity right now.

Perhaps she could get their supper ready and surprise him. Maybe if she could show him how useful she was he would let her stay anyway?

But she couldn't find the steak Josh had said he wanted,

the fridge was more or less empty, so that put paid to that idea.

She was feeling hot, sticky and bad-tempered, her near future uncertain, all depending on the whim of a man who could be lazily charming but who could also be forcefully arrogant, even a little cruel at times.

She went back to the bedroom, taking fresh clothes out of her case, the denims and top she had on now all dusty from the drive here. Oh, to hell with it, she would have a shower! Josh was apparently too busy to even talk to her, and she had nothing else to do.

It was glorious! She cooled the water down to lukewarm, revelling in it, her skin tingling refreshingly, her wet hair plastered to her brow. There had been some shampoo in the bathroom cabinet, not her usual brand, but it would do.

She was just massaging the shampoo into a lather when she heard the shower door click open. She turned, blinking, shampoo instantly going into her eyes and blinding her, stinging the sensative tissue there.

'Josh?' she gasped, reaching out blindly.

'It sure is,' he drawled.

'I—Help me,' she pleaded. 'I have soap in my eyes and—and—Are you looking at me?' she asked in dismay.

'Nowhere else to look, honey.'

She could hear the smile in his voice, and her face coloured bright red. 'Will you get me a towel, you—you ogling idiot!' She would die of embarrassment in a minute!

He chuckled. 'I have a much better idea,' he murmured throatily.

The shower door clicked shut. Heavens, he had gone and left her! Then she felt heated flesh pressed against her arm, hard male flesh, and those long, tanned hands came up to cleanse the soap from her hair and eyes.

'Better?' Josh asked softly.

Her eyes weren't stinging any more, but nevertheless,

she didn't open them. 'Go away,' she pleaded shakily. 'Please, I—I—You shouldn't have come in here.'

'I heard the shower and thought it might be fun to join you. It is. Open your eyes, Erin.'

'I—No!' She shook her head, the feel of Josh's body against hers making her tremble, the coolness of her skin now a flaming heat.

'Open your eyes!' he ordered in an inflexible voice.

She did so, reluctantly, instantly closing them again until she heard him chuckle. She glared up at him rebelliously, willing herself not to blush, but knowing she had.

Josh was as wet as she was now, his hair glossily black, his wide shoulders tanned a deep mahogany, as was the rest of him. Dark hair grew thick and silky on his chest, tapering down to his waist. That was as far as Erin's gaze dared go—as far as it could go, the lower halves of their bodies were moulded together!

'You should have let me know you were going to have a shower—I would have enjoyed soaping you all over,' he grinned down at her, water running in rivulets down his face.

Her hands pushed ineffectually at his chest. 'Please, Josh, you have to leave, or I will. I——' Her words were cut off as Josh lifted her high in the air, lowering her body so that he could catch one erect nipple in his waiting lips. 'No . . .' she groaned as pleasure hit every nerve in her body.

If Josh heard her protest he didn't heed it, but transferred his mouth to the other taut nipple, teasing it with his tongue and teeth.

Erin's hands rested on his shoulders, her head thrown back in wonder. Slowly Josh lowered her until their lips met and clung, holding her high against him, as if she weighed nothing at all, his arms like steel bands.

He still kissed her as he shouldered his way out of the shower, water dripping off their wet bodies as he carried her over to the bed, covering her body with his after laying her back against the downy bedclothes.

His lips moved to her throat, probing the deep hollows there, nibbling gently on the skin. His hands slowly caressed her from breast to thigh, lingering over the latter, as if he desired to know each intimate inch of her.

For Erin time had ceased to exist; Josh's body on hers, and the magic his lips were evoking, was all she could think of at the moment, her silky limbs entwined with his rougher ones, the throbbing urgency of his body telling her more than words could ever do.

Josh seemed to be of the same opinion. 'You're a silent lover, Erin,' he said huskily, 'but I like that.' He began a slow descent of her body, leaving a trail of fire wherever his lips touched, rewarding each ruby-red peak of her breasts with a long lingering caress of his sensuous mouth, exploring the tautness of her stomach with a thoroughness that had her squirming with pleasure.

'Josh!' she gasped, grasping his head to pull him back up to her. 'No more, Josh,' she begged. 'I—I can't stand it!'

'All right, sweetheart,' he gave her a heart-stopping smile. 'I only wanted to give you pleasure.'

'And you did——'

'It isn't over yet,' he told her huskily, caressing her breast as he kissed her.

Erin wrenched her head away. 'It *is* over, Josh. It has to be.'

'Don't be ridiculous, Erin,' he chided gently. 'You and I have a lot of loving to do yet. We——'

'Josh, Bob was my stepfather!' she burst out. '*Just* my stepfather.' There, it was said!

Josh froze, slowly lifting his head to look at her, his gaze ravaging the darkness of her eyes, the paleness of her face. 'Your stepfather?' he repeated slowly.

Erin swallowed hard. 'Yes.'

'Just your stepfather.'

'Yes.' Her breathing was shallow.

'And after your mother died you lived with him for a year?' He seemed to be having trouble speaking, a pulse working erratically in his jaw.

'Yes,' she acknowledged softly.

He closed his eyes, taking a deep breath before he levered himself to his feet. His expression was scornful as she turned away. 'A little late for modesty,' he drawled, walking away.

She looked at him with shadowed eyes, flushing as she registered what a magnificent body he had, wide powerful shoulders, tapered waist and hips, his thighs powerfully muscled, his legs long and covered with fine dark hair. He was so handsome she almost choked with it.

'Where are you going?' she croaked.

He turned to grimace. 'Back in the shower—cold this time. And if you have any sense you'll have got your clothes and yourself the hell out of my bedroom before I return!'

CHAPTER FIVE

ERIN must have set a record for dressing, hastily pulling on the clean clothing she had taken out for herself before going into the shower, the clothes clinging to her damply in the absence of a towel to finish drying herself.

She could still hear the shower running as she left the room, taking her case into one of the other bedrooms. After all, Josh hadn't told her to leave the house, just his bedroom.

Facing him again was going to be embarrassing, there could be no denying that, but it had to be done. She was through running away from situations. And she had walked into this one with her eyes open.

She wandered through to the lounge. Fire—she could smell fire! And, oh God, she could see smoke! The house was on fire!

'Josh!' She ran back to the bedroom, pulling the shower door open. 'Josh——'

He scowled down at her. 'What the hell do you want now?'

'Josh, the house is on fire!' She got hold of his arm and began pulling him towards the lounge.

'It's *what*?' he thundered, sparing time to pull a towel about his hips before following her. His eyes narrowed as he looked around the orderly room. 'Where?'

'Not in here!' her eyes were wild. 'Out there,' she pointed to where she had seen the smoke billowing out seconds earlier.

'Out there?' he asked patiently.

'Yes—come and look. Honestly, Josh, I would have

thought you'd be a little more interested in the fact that
your home is on fire! Come on!' she pulled at his arm once
again.

He gave her a pitying glance. 'No, you come and look.'
He led the way, opening the door to the covered patio
area. 'There's your fire.'

Colour flooded her cheeks as she looked at the steaming
barbecue standing out on the concrete area, the hot coals
getting wet from the light summer rain falling.

'I lit it for the steaks,' Josh explained as if talking to a
backward child. 'But I got—sidetracked,' he taunted,
shutting the door. 'The rain has put an end to that idea.'

'Oh.' Erin looked down at her hands, feeling an absolute
idiot. Why on earth hadn't she checked the source of the
smoke before running to Josh? 'I'm sorry, Josh,' she
muttered. 'I really thought the house was on fire.' She
looked up at him with pleading eyes.

His mouth quirked into a smile, the glower leaving his
eyes as he seemed to relax. 'You really are the most amaz-
ing girl I've ever met,' he laughed. 'I know one thing, the
next two weeks aren't going to be boring.'

Her eyes widened hopefully. 'You mean you're going to
let me stay?'

'Sure,' he shrugged resignedly. 'I may make the occasional pass at you, but I did warn you about the sexual
harassment before you came here.'

'Yes, you did,' and she grinned her relief that he wasn't
going to just throw her out.

Josh quirked one dark eyebrow. 'Think you can handle
it?'

'I can try.'

His arm went about her shoulders. 'You might even
enjoy it, hmm?'

She blushed, remembering her unmistakable response
earlier. 'I might.'

'I know damn well I will.' He moved away from her, slapping her lightly on the bottom. 'I've brought the steaks in from the truck, you'll find them in the kitchen. Get to work, woman.'

'Yes, sir,' she agreed lightly.

She set to work with a light heart. The steaks were now in the refrigerator with various other foods. Cooking certainly didn't seem to be Josh's speciality; frozen vegetables and packets of french-fries filled most of the freezer section of the fridge. She used some of the contents for convenience, as the evening was getting late, but she wouldn't make a habit of it.

Josh came back wearing a clean checked shirt and denims, and sat down at the breakfast bar. 'Smells good,' he said appreciatively.

'I—I hope so,' she bit her lip. 'The cooker—er—stove is a bit strange to me.'

He stood up to look at the cooking food. 'Looks good too. Is it going to be long?'

'About five minutes, I should think.'

He grinned. 'But you aren't sure?'

'No,' she pulled a face.

He sat down again, drinking the coffee she had poured for him. 'Do you want to talk now or later?' He looked at her steadily.

Erin paled. 'Talk?'

He nodded. 'You can see that we have to.'

'We do?'

'I'm afraid so,' he derided. 'The situation has changed, surely you realise that?'

'Because I'll no longer be sleeping with you?'

'Mm,' he agreed dryly. 'I'd looked forward to a couple of weeks of you sharing my bed, now I have to think of something else to do with you.'

'I'll still clean and cook for you,' Erin put in hastily,

finding this conversation embarrassing to say the least.

'Yes,' he laughed. 'But I'm sure you'll agree that there isn't enough of either of them to merit the—wage you'll be earning?'

'No,' she agreed ruefully, well aware of how much her air ticket must have cost. 'So what do you want me to do?' She bit her lip. 'If you still want me, even though you'll be the first, I——'

'No,' he cut in firmly. 'Save that for the man you love. No, I have an idea of what you can do but—Honey, there's smoke coming out of the stove!'

They both rushed over to open the door, and Josh pulled out the tray that contained the steaks. 'Never mind,' he viewed the burnt offering, 'I like my steaks well done.'

'Really?'

'Yes, really,' he teased.

'*That* well done?' Erin grimaced at the shrunken steaks.

'Well . . .' he grinned, 'easy on the burning next time, hmm?'

She smiled back. 'I'll try,' she promised.

'Then let's eat.' He went to the fridge. 'Like a beer? Or some wine, I think I have some somewhere. Sharon used to like it.'

Sharon, Dave's dead fiancée, and Josh's—what? His dead *love*? 'I think I'll just have water, thanks,' she refused stiffly.

The steak was so burnt it crunched, the french fries were somehow greasy, and the peas were mushy, but Josh ate it without complaint.

'You'll do better tomorrow,' he sympathised as she left most of hers on the plate.

'I hope so. Josh, earlier, after—after you walked out on me, did you go upstairs?'

'Mm.'

She licked her lips, her curiosity getting the better of

her. Josh was just as likely to slap her down again if she got too inquisitive. 'Why?'

He sighed. 'You'll have to know some time, so it might as well be now. Come with me and I'll show you.' He stood up.

'If you'd rather not——' and she hung back.

He shrugged. 'You have to know anyway, if you're to agree to my suggestion.'

'Your—suggestion has to do with your work?'

'Yes.' He held out his hand to her

She confidently put her own inside it, curling her fingers about his taut flesh. Sheba lay at the bottom of the stairs as if guarding the contents of the room above her.

Josh grinned as the dog seemed to raise an eyebrow enquiringly at them. 'Don't mind her. She's sulking because I never allow her upstairs with me.'

Erin warily stepped over the dog, following Josh's example. 'Maybe she won't like me going up there with you.' The last thing she wanted was for the dog to dislike her—any more than she seemed to already!

'She can take it,' he chuckled.

The attic-room, although in a bungalow she supposed it couldn't really be called that, covered the whole floor space of the four bedrooms and two bathrooms—and its contents came as a complete shock to her. It was a studio! An artist's studio, easels, both used and unused standing about the room. The walls themselves were bare, except for one large painting, a painting of a girl, a girl with dark hair and laughing brown eyes. Sharon!

Josh walked straight over to the portrait, as if he too were drawn to it like a magnet. 'My one and only painting of Sharon,' he spoke as if to himself. 'And even then I painted it after she died.' His voice was raw with emotion.

'I—It's very good,' Erin said awkwardly, wondering if Dave had ever seen this painting, seen the love that had gone into every brush stroke.

'Yes,' Josh acknowledged without conceit. 'She was a good subject to paint—as I think you will be.'

She gasped. 'You want to paint *me*?'

He nodded. 'I even have a title for it: *Innocence*.'

She flushed. 'I—My God, you're Hawke!' she gasped, having seen the signature at the bottom of Sharon's portrait for the first time. She looked almost dazedly at Josh. 'You're Hawke,' she repeated weakly, wondering why she didn't faint or something.

Green eyes narrowed warily. 'You've heard of me?'

Heard of him? She had admired his paintings for years, ever since she had seen a picture of one in a book at school. He usually painted the mountains of Canada or its snowy wasteland, but the ones she liked best were the ones of the Canadian Indians, the proud people of yesterday seeming to come alive under his brush.

Now she knew the reason for his wealth, the reason Martha had seemed so surprised when she had asked if he were a rancher. This man was a genius, a veritable giant among artists.

'Why on earth were you staying in that dump of a motel?' she blurted out the first thing that came into her mind, staring at him with awestruck eyes.

His mouth twisted. 'I hate being recognised. At a large hotel the chances of that are quite high—believe it or not, I'm quite highly thought of in this country.'

'Not only in Canada, in the whole world. I can hardly believe I'm actually talking to you!' Erin shook her head.

Josh quirked a mocking eyebrow. 'I'm still the same man you just ate dinner with,' he taunted her sudden awe. 'And I'm still the same man who wanted to go to bed with you,' he added mockingly.

Colour flamed her cheeks. 'I know that, it's just—I just love your paintings!' Her eyes glowed. 'I had a couple of your prints at home, but I had to leave them behind,' she explained sadly.

'Which couple?'

'Don't you believe me?' she bristled.

He held up his hands defensively. 'I only asked, Erin.'

'Sorry,' she muttered. 'I had *Sunset* and *Indian Land*.'

He nodded. 'Two of my own favourites. Well, now you can be a Hawke original.'

Erin paled. 'You want to paint me?'

'Yes.'

'Goodness!' she gasped. 'It's such an honour—I don't know what to say. You——'

'You haven't heard yet how I want to paint you, Erin,' he put in softly.

'I—How?'

'Nude.'

'N-Nude?' she repeated faintly.

'Yes.'

She swallowed hard, her hands twisting together in front of her. 'Without my clothes on?' she said jerkily.

Josh's mouth quirked mockingly. 'That's usually what nude means, yes. I'm sure you'll agree that your plane ticket is a big enough fee.'

'I should think most women would pay *you*.'

'I don't want "most women",' he said softly. 'I want you.'

He meant it, he really meant it. Joshua Hawke wanted to paint her nude! She couldn't do it, of course she couldn't do it. The idea was unthinkable.

'I wouldn't touch you, Erin,' he told her softly. 'When I paint I'm completely absorbed in my work.'

'*That* absorbed?' She couldn't believe that the man who had shown her so much passion earlier this evening could switch his emotions off so completely.

He laughed softly. 'I don't know about when I'm paint-

ing a nude, I've never painted one before. But if I touch
vou I won't be able to call it *Innocence*, will I?'

Colour flooded her cheeks once again. 'No . . .'

'Then is it a deal?' His gaze was intent.

'I—I don't think I could,' she pulled a face. 'Not nude.'

'I could always paint it from memory,' he drawled.

'Josh——'

'But I would rather not,' he continued as if she hadn't
spoken. 'I'm sure your body can't be as good as I remember
it.' He gave a rueful smile. 'Right now I have such a vision
in my mind . . .! I want the true picture, not one from my
imagination. So, will you do it?'

'I—What if I don't?'

'I never think in negatives,' Josh dismissed.

'Is that why you told Dave to expect my call?' His
certainty about that still rankled.

He raised one dark eyebrow. 'Would you rather he
hadn't known who you were? Would you rather have had
to make the explanations?'

'No. But——'

'I don't deal in "ifs" or "buts" either, Erin. I told Dave
to expect your call because I wanted you to make it, not
because I *expected* you to. If you hadn't . . .' he shrugged.
'But you did. And you're here, and now I want to paint
you. You'll be a first for me, Erin.'

'I know I should be flattered, I just——'

'You're just not sure you can do it,' he finished patiently,
standing up. 'Well, think about it and let me know tomorrow.'

'Tomorrow . . .?'

'Sure,' Josh nodded. 'We only have two weeks, Erin. If
I'm to get it finished in time for my exhibition in London
we have to get started tomorrow.'

'Your exhibition?' Her eyes were wide. 'So that's why
you're going to England. Were they your paintings you

had in that crate yesterday?'

'Yes. Now, do you have an answer now or shall I wait until the morning?'

She bit her bottom lip. 'Can I—can I let you know in the morning?'

'I guess,' he sighed. 'I'll see you later.'

Erin gave him a startled look. 'Where are you going?'

'To take Sheba out for her evening walk. Do you want to come with us?'

She remembered the way the boisterous dog jumped about all over the place, the wide jaws and long teeth still making her nervous. 'I think I'll stay here and tidy the kitchen.'

'Okay,' he shrugged, leaving her.

Pose nude! Could she possibly do something like that? Surely it was better than the original idea of sharing Josh's bed?

It still shocked her to think of him as the painter Hawke. She just hadn't made the connection between the lazily attractive man she knew him to be and the world-famous painter. He had been acknowledged as a genius for the last ten years, which meant he had only been twenty-four when he found his fame. He seemed to have handled his fame well, in a very mature way, managing to maintain normality in his private life.

Now could she be mature? Josh was an artist, she would simply be a subject to him. But would she? He seemed to think so. But the memory of their passionate encounter kept coming back to taunt her.

She could hear Sheba barking in the distance as she settled down in the lounge, switching on the television and half-heartedly watching the American comedy now showing.

It didn't hold her attention, and she moved restlessly about the room, hearing a strange 'yip-yip' noise coming from somewhere outside. She had never heard such a noise before, and for some reason it made her feel tense.

Where on earth was Josh? Surely Sheba had had enough of a walk for one night? He shouldn't have left her alone here like this, there could be anything out there in the darkness. A bear, or a wolf, or——The sound of the front door opening had her running to greet Josh.

She launched herself into his arms, uncaring of his surprise, knocking his hat off his head as she clung to him. 'Thank goodness you're back!' she breathed her relief against his chest.

'What the hell——! What's wrong with you, Erin?' He put her away from him, bending down to pick up his hat and throw it in a cupboard.

She was once again feeling foolish. 'I—You were gone so long. I——'

'I was gone fifteen minutes,' he derided, taking off his jacket and throwing it in the cupboard with his hat.

Erin looked down awkwardly at her hands, embarrassed now by her show of fear. 'It just seemed longer,' she muttered. 'Where's Sheba?'

'She doesn't sleep in the house. She's basically a guard dog.'

'Oh,' she nodded, suddenly frowning. 'Guard dog against what?'

Josh shrugged, strolling through to the lounge, Erin at his heels. 'We get the occasional wildlife around here, and we have been known to have prowlers.'

The mention of the wildlife interested her more than the latter. 'You mean bears, and wolves, and—things?' Her eyes were wide with apprehension.

'No,' he laughed. 'We don't get bears here, wolves either for that matter. The occasional coyote and——'

'Coyote?' she repeated sharply. 'You get *coyotes* here?'

'Yep,' he grinned at her shock. 'You don't have them in

South London, hmm?' he taunted.

'No,' she shuddered. 'Was that them I heard, that strange noise?'

'Probably,' he nodded.

'Heavens!'

'There's no need to be scared,' he put his arm about her shoulders. 'Coyotes don't bother humans.'

'Are you sure?'

'Very,' he chuckled. 'Now get to bed, I don't want my model looking tired.'

Colour flooded her cheeks. 'You think I'll do it, then?' she said challengingly.

'Won't you?' he quirked an eyebrow.

'I—Yes,' she admitted grudgingly. 'I don't have any choice, do I?'

'Everyone has a choice, Erin.' His expression was grim. 'Go to bed. And don't forget our ride in the morning.'

'Er—Our ride?'

'Mm,' he nodded. 'You haven't forgotten?'

'Oh no, no, of course not. I—I'm looking forward to it,' she lied. Help, he was actually expecting her to get on a horse in the morning!

'So am I,' he smiled. 'About seven, okay?'

'Fine,' she nodded airily, quickly making her escape.

Oh dear, not only was she to pose nude tomorrow but she was to ride a horse first!

She couldn't sleep, was sure she hadn't slept at all when Josh knocked on her bedroom door the next morning.

'Six-thirty, Erin,' he called cheerfully. 'Time to get up.'

'Okay,' she agreed grumpily, snuggling further down into the covers, just longing to go back to sleep.

'Now, Erin!' warned Josh as if guessing her intention.

She sat up abruptly. 'I said okay,' she snapped.

'So you did,' he chuckled. 'I'll go and make a pot of

coffee, you sound like you could use some.' He went off whistling.

Erin scowled at the closed door. No one had the right to be that cheerful first thing in the morning! Still, she should be looking on the bright side; at least she didn't have to clean forty rooms this morning, and she didn't have to fight off Mike Johnston's lecherous hands either. But she did have to pose nude for Josh, and she had agreed to go riding with him this morning. It was the former that had kept her awake most of the night, but it was the latter that was now prominent in her mind.

Josh knocked on the door again five minutes later as she was pulling on her denims. 'Coffee's in the kitchen. I'll be outside saddling the horses when you're ready.'

Her heart gave a sickening lurch at the thought of it. 'Fine. I—I'll be out shortly.'

'No hurry,' and he went off whistling again.

Erin slumped down on the bed. What if the horse should bolt with her? What if it should rear up and throw her? Maybe she should tell Josh that she had never ridden before, and that the sheer thought of getting up on one's back terrified the life out of her. Even as she thought of it she knew she couldn't tell him. He had probably been around horses all his life, he wouldn't understand her fears.

She was in the kitchen sipping coffee when he came back into the house, his narrow-eyed gaze taking in the denims, tee-shirt, and flat shoes she wore at a glance.

'Ready?'

She looked up at him. Now was the time to tell him, now before it was too late. But her body seemed to have other ideas, and she stood up, words coming out of her mouth without any conscious thought on her part. 'Yes, I'm ready.'

'The horses are rarin' to go,' he grinned, holding the door open for her.

Oh lord! 'Good,' she heard herself say woodenly.

Josh swung easily on to the back of the black stallion, at once seeming to become one with the horse. Erin looked at the quieter gelding she was to ride, and the gelding eyed her straight back!

'Er—what's his name?' she asked nervously.

'Blaize,' Josh supplied.

She wasn't even sure how to get up into the saddle. It had looked so easy when Josh did it, but the stirrup now looked so high to her.

'Like a leg up?' Josh offered.

She swallowed hard, feeling a sheen of perspiration break out on her top lip. 'I—Perhaps that might be best.' She watched as he swung down to the ground, couldn't help but admire his easy familiarity with the two horses.

It seemed that within seconds Josh had hoisted her up into the saddle, the ground looking a long way down as she clung on.

Josh handed her the reins. 'How do the stirrups feel?' He looked up at her enquiringly.

'Er—feel?' She was afraid to move, terrified she was going to fall off any second.

'Are they the right length?' he explained patiently.

'Oh—er—yes,' she nodded frantically, not having the faintest idea whether they were or not. Her feet were in them, and that was good enough for her.

'Good.' Josh swung back up on to the stallion's back. 'Follow me for a while. And no fancy tricks, Blaize doesn't like it.' He set the stallion off at a steady walk, holding back on the reins as the stallion baulked at such a sedate pace.

No fancy tricks! Erin couldn't even get the damned

horse to move! She just sat there on its back while it chewed merrily on the grass at its feet.

Josh turned in his saddle. 'They can eat when they get back,' he told her.

She tentatively pulled on the reins, amazed as the proud head came up. Now what did she do? Josh had given his horse a gentle dig in the ribs. Fantastic! It worked! Blaize moved off at a slow walk, slowly catching Josh and the stallion up.

Hey, she thought, this wasn't half bad. The horse seemed docile enough, and the gentle rocking movement was quite pleasant. Yes, she could get to quite like this—and she might have to.

They were walking along a worn trail through the wood at the back of the house, the peace and quiet relaxing Erin even more in the saddle, Blaize seeming quite content to follow where the stallion led.

'If we're lucky we may see some deer,' Josh turned to say softly.

'Really?' She couldn't keep the excitement out of her voice.

'Mm. Better than coyotes, hmm?' he teased.

Erin didn't bother to answer him, and her tension suddenly returned as Blaize seemed to stumble on one of the large stones that littered their way. She was sure she must have gone white as for a moment it seemed the horse would fall. He didn't, but her fear was back, stronger than before, her body rigid in the saddle.

'How far are we going?' she asked Josh in a casual voice.

'Just a couple of miles.'

A couple of *miles*! The hardness of the saddle was already beginning to hurt the inside of her thighs; two miles of this and she doubted she would be able to walk!

When they emerged on the other side of the wood Josh began to trot the stallion. Erin knew she was in trouble when Blaize once again followed the stallion's lead, breaking into a steady gallop to catch up, further increasing her discomfort.

It was the weirdest sensation of her life, feeling as if her whole body were being shaken apart. Josh seemed to flow with the horse, whereas she felt as if any moment all her teeth were going to be rattled from her mouth. And she felt sure she was going to fall off. Her feet in the stirrups said she wouldn't, but her knees were shaking so much she was finding it difficult to hang on.

Finally they had crossed the clearing, and Josh slowed his horse down to a walk again as they went back into the woods. Erin's relief was such that she was glad just to still be on Blaize's back; the gentle rocking movement felt like heaven.

'Isn't everywhere beautiful this time of morning?' Josh grinned as he reined the stallion in next to the gelding.

'Lovely,' she agreed wanly, concentrating so hard on staying on that she daren't even look up at him.

'You don't sound too sure. Want to turn back?'

'Heavens, no!' She looked up to give him a bright smile. 'I'm really enjoying this,' she lied.

'Well, if you're sure . . .? It must be some time since you last rode.'

'A while,' she nodded. 'But I'm fine, really.'

'Okay,' Josh shrugged. 'Just say when you've had enough.'

She gritted her teeth and hung on for grim death, determined not to be the one to call a halt to this ride. It was almost an hour later when Josh finally said they should turn back, an hour that seemed like a lifetime to Erin, an hour when her whole body seemed to ache, her knees actually going numb. And they had to go back yet!

For some reason the ride back seemed shorter, although each step the horse took seemed like agony to Erin, and her inner thighs now felt red-raw from the hardness of the leather saddle.

Josh swung easily to the ground once they were back in the corral, coming over to Erin as she tried to do the same, her knees giving way as soon as her feet made contact with the ground.

'Steady!' Josh grasped her arm to balance her.

She felt as if she were still sitting astride the saddle, her legs strangely bowed as she clung to Josh, her inner thighs starting to sting now.

'How do you feel?' he grinned down at her, his hat pushed to the back of his head, his hair dark and unruly.

'Er—Fine.' She made an effort to stand up on her own, amazed when she actually managed to do it.

'Sure?'

'I said I was fine!' she snapped. 'Sorry,' she muttered. 'I—I must have been out of practice after all.' She brushed down her denims.

'I guess,' Josh nodded, his amusement deepening.

Erin gave him a suspicious look. 'Josh . . .?'

'Mm?' He looked strangely innocent.

Which was a contradiction in itself! This man was rakishly attractive, very physical, and there wasn't a single innocent thing about him.

Her mouth set in an angry line, her discomfort suddenly forgotten as she glared at him with accusing eyes. 'You knew!' she exploded. 'You knew, damn you!'

He began unsaddling the stallion. 'Knew what, Erin?' he asked in that still innocent voice, eyeing her mockingly.

She drew in an angry breath. 'God, you lousy, rotten, stinking——!' Her words were cut off as Josh pulled her to him, parting her lips with his own. She was too angry to respond, pounding at his chest with her fists.

'Hey,' he held her away from him. 'It was only a joke——'

'A joke!' she snorted. 'Oh yes, very funny!' She wrenched away from him, her eyes sparkling like jewels. 'I'm almost crippled for life and you did it for a joke! And you can stop laughing!' She stamped her foot furiously, and the ache in her knee protested at such treatment. 'I could have fallen off,' she accused. 'I could have been hurt, and you did it for a *joke!*' Her voice rose hysterically, her fears very real.

Josh looked unimpressed. 'You were in no danger——'

'No danger?' she repeated in a loud voice. 'I was absolutely terrified, and you say there was no danger!'

'Erin——'

'Don't you "Erin" me!' She shook off his hand on her arm. 'I think you're the lowest, most contemptible creep I've ever had the misfortune to meet. Lower even than Mike Johnston!' came her parting shot as she marched off into the house.

Josh made no effort to follow her, which was perhaps as well, she would probably have hit him if he had said another word to her.

He had done it on purpose, had made her suffer the torture of sitting on that horse for almost two hours when he had known all the time that she had never ridden before. She could have been killed, could have—— But she knew she exaggerated. Blaize had been the gentlest of horses, completely docile.

But, heavens, she ached! And *that* was Josh's fault.

She was slumped down on the bed when the knock sounded on the door. 'What do you want?' she asked crossly, and sat up straight, determined not to show any sign of weakness in front of Josh.

His expression was bland as he opened the door. 'I want to get to work,' he told her abruptly.

She stood up, moving stiffly. 'Then you'll have to wait.

I smell of horses, I want to have a bath.'

'Make it a shower,' he said tersely. 'I want to get started this morning.'

'I haven't said I'll definitely do it yet,' she reminded him tautly.

'You will. I'll be upstairs when you're ready.' He closed the door forcefully as he left.

He was so damned sure of himself! And what was he so angry about? She was the one who had been made to look a fool. But his anger had put her on the defensive, so much so that she was determined to thwart him.

She had never realised what a pungent smell horses had, but the smell seemed to be clinging to her clothes, and while it wasn't an unpleasant odour, it wasn't exactly pleasant either. Oh, damn Joshua Hawke, she would have her bath if she wanted one. She had told him he could wait, and that was exactly what he could do.

The water was deliciously refreshing, coloured lightly blue by the bath-salts she had found in the bathroom cabinet. They had a flowery aroma, so they didn't belong to Josh. Sharon's name instantly sprang to mind.

Just how close had Josh been to the other woman? And why had she committed suicide? No one had told her that. Could it be that her love for two men had been too much for her?

Both men were attractive in their own way, although to her mind Josh came out in front. Had Sharon thought so too, and been afraid to tell Dave so only a month before their wedding?

But surely suicide was a drastic step to take for such a predicament? She considered suicide a strong step to take in any situation.

Sharon had been lucky, she didn't just love two men, she had two men who loved her in return. Surely the situation could have been resolved without such a drastic—

and to Erin's mind, wasteful—conclusion.

The bathroom door suddenly swung open with a crash, and Josh stood dark and dangerous in the doorway. 'I thought I told you not to take a bath,' he rasped.

Her hands moved to cover her breasts, not even having any bubbles on top of the water to hide her nakedness. Not that Josh seemed concerned with that; he stood there looking at her dispassionately.

'Get out of here!' she ordered indignantly, two high spots of colour in her cheeks.

'I'll go when I'm good and ready.' He came to stand at the side of the bath. 'Now when I tell you I want to work, that's exactly what I want to do,' he ground out. 'And I don't like to be kept waiting.'

'I told you I was having a bath. You——'

'And *I* told *you* that you didn't have the time for one.' He wrenched her chin up so that she had no choice but to look at him. 'Now you get your butt out of that bath and up to my studio, pronto.' His fingers bit into the softness of her skin before he let her go. 'You understand?' he said curtly.

He was good and mad, much angrier than she had been minutes earlier. 'I—I understand,' she nodded nervously.

His mouth twisted. 'If you aren't up in the studio in five minutes I'll come and get you.'

'I'll be there,' she assured him hastily.

'I'm sure you will,' he drawled before leaving.

CHAPTER SIX

FOR the first time in days Erin felt genuinely hungry—and she knew she daren't even take the time to get herself a slice of toast. Josh had been pretty emphatic, and she knew he meant every word.

She hurriedly towelled herself dry, donning a light blue cotton sun-top and matching shorts. The sun was already quite hot, and would probably be even more so up in the studio, where the roof seemed to consist mainly of windows, providing plenty of natural light for Josh to work by.

He had a fresh canvas set up on the easel when she entered the room, and a sheet of royal-blue velvet was draped across a sofa a few feet in front of him.

Erin stood nervously just inside the door, waiting for him to notice her, his attention seemingly inwards.

Suddenly he turned, his gaze impersonal as it flickered over her. 'I'm ready for you now,' he said curtly.

She licked her lips. 'I—Where shall I undress?'

He shrugged. 'It doesn't really matter. Anywhere.'

'I—er—Don't you have a screen or something?'

'Nope. I've never needed one before. My first nude, remember,' he said dryly.

'Yes.' She looked down at her hands. 'I—I'll get undressed over here, shall I?' She moved behind a chair that stood at the back of him.

'Anywhere,' he said tersely. 'Just hurry up and do it.'

'There's no need to be nasty,' she choked, slipping out of the cotton shorts, leaving her black lacy briefs on for the moment. 'It may be your first nude,' she muttered, pulling off the sun-top to reveal the black bra that matched the briefs, 'but this is the first time I've *posed* in the nude too!'

'Just get on with it, Erin,' he sighed.

She hesitated about removing any more clothing. 'Could I keep my bra and briefs on?' she pleaded.

He turned to look at her, impatience etched into his hard features. 'Get them off, Erin. And quickly, before I come over there and do it for you.'

'All right,' she snapped. 'But I think I hate you.'

'Is that supposed to bother me?' He pulled up a chair, putting it next to the easel before sitting on it, a sketch-pad in his hands.

She flung her bra down on the chair with the rest of her clothing, sure that she was blushing all over her body. 'I don't just think I hate you, I *know* I do.' God, she had never felt so—so *naked* before!

'Over to the couch, Erin,' Josh instructed curtly. 'Today I'll just be deciding on a pose and doing some sketches. We'll get down to some actual painting tomorrow.'

'Posing' turned out to be the most humiliating experience of her life. Josh moved her into every conceivable position, touching each part of her body as if she were no more than an inanimate piece of clay.

And maybe to him she was! But she had never been touched like this, not even when he had been making love to her. And his criticism of her was even harder to bear.

'Don't droop your shoulders like that,' he instructed once. Or, 'Arch your legs, Erin, they look slimmer that way.' As if she had fat legs! And then there was, 'Don't bend your head in that way, it gives you a double chin.'

'Is there anything about my body you *do* like?' she finally asked crossly.

'You have good skin, nice breasts, and fine bones,' he returned absently, debating whether or not to have her hair forward on her shoulders or pulled back to show her features. He left it loose on her shoulders, stepping back to study the effect.

'Fine bones!' Erin exploded.

'Yes—Don't move!' he snapped impatiently. 'I've spent half an hour getting you in the right position.'

Had it only been half an hour? It had seemed like a lifetime! Her nudity seemed to mean nothing to Josh, and after a while it had come to mean nothing to her either. But she didn't like being just the owner of good skin, nice breasts, and fine bones! She was a person, not an object, and she wouldn't put up with this insulting behaviour a minute longer. Even the pose he had finally settled on was degrading, having her kneeling on the floor on the blue velvet cover, her arms outstretched as if longing for someone to love her. The painting might be going to be titled *Innocence*, but the pose seemed to say she wouldn't be that for much longer.

She stood up, moving silently to the chair to begin putting her clothes back on.

Josh watched her with narrowed eyes. 'What do you think you're doing?'

'Guess!' she snapped, her clothes giving her confidence once again.

'We have some sketches to do.'

'I've had enough——'

'Enough of what?' he rasped.

She shrugged. 'Enough of this, enough of you, enough of——'

'Degrading yourself? Have you had enough of that, Erin?' he asked tautly.

She gave him a sharp look. 'I—You—What are you talking about?'

'I'm talking about you, Erin. I'm talking about the way you agreed to leave town with a complete stranger, how you didn't even know *where* you were going, how you agreed to have a sexual relationship with that complete stranger.' He walked over to her, shaking her angrily by the shoulders. 'That's what the hell I'm talking about, Erin! I'm talking about *you*, and the lack of respect you seem to have for yourself and your body. Do you have any idea of the sort of trouble you could have landed yourself in?'

She looked down at the dark hair on his chest just visible beneath his unbuttoned shirt, unable to look any higher, physically whipped by his verbal onslaught. 'You seemed kind——'

'I could have been a raving lunatic for all you know!' He shook her again. 'Kind!' he raised his eyes heaven-wards. 'I seemed *kind*? When I'd made it clear you would be sharing a bed with me, that I intended making love to you?'

'But you haven't——'

'No, I haven't, have I?' he agreed grimly.

Erin looked up, searching his harsh features. 'Was this nude posing another joke, Josh? Like this morning's amusing little incident?' She wrenched out of his grasp. 'Was it, Josh?'

'No, it damn well wasn't!' His eyes were like chips of ice. 'It wasn't a joke at all, it was meant to bring you back to your senses. If you hadn't told me I would be the first with you I would have made love to you, do you realise that?'

'I—Yes. But you didn't.'

'No, because I figured that one of us lacking respect for you was enough,' he scorned.

'You—you—you bastard!' Her hand shot out and she struck him hard across one lean cheek.

She wasn't prepared for the way Josh's arm rose as he hit her with the back of his hand, and she staggered back with the force of the blow. Her eyes were wide with pain as she held her throbbing cheek.

'I hate you!' she choked before running out of the room, for once not nervous of Sheba as she ran past the dog to her room, locking the door behind her.

She couldn't remember anyone ever hitting her before, not her mother, and certainly not her stepfather. But Josh had seemed to do it without conscious thought, hurting her as much by committing the act as he had by the actual force of the blow.

She jumped nervously as the door-handle was turned, the door rattling as the lock prevented it from opening.

'Erin! Erin, open the door,' Josh requested softly.

She made no answer. She never intended speaking to him again, was going to leave here and she hoped never set eyes on him again.

'Erin!' he repeated patiently. 'Let me in, honey.'

His use of the endearment almost had her giving him an angry retort, but she managed to restrain herself. She wouldn't give him the satisfaction of talking to him.

'Would it help if I said I was sorry?' His question was once again met with silence. 'I'm just going to make lunch,' he added enticingly. 'Want some?'

Did she! She was feeling really hungry. But she wouldn't give in. She was glad that she hadn't unpacked her things, it would save her the trouble of having to repack.

'Sure?' he coaxed. 'Bacon and eggs, an Englishman's— or in this case, woman's—dream, or so I'm told.'

Bacon and eggs! Her mouth watered just at the thought of them. But she wouldn't give in.

'No?' Josh said regretfully. 'Well, I'll leave Sheba outside your door in case you feel like company.' He could be heard instructing the obedient dog to 'stay' before his foot-steps went off in the direction of the kitchen.

Damn him! Was there nothing that man didn't know about her? He had guessed she intended leaving and had left Sheba outside to make sure she didn't. Surely he could see they had nothing left to say to one another, that they had both said, and done, too much already?

Apparently not, and she could hear him whistling tunelessly from the kitchen. The smell of bacon cooking soon wafted over to her side of the house, a torture in itself. Her stomach grumbled protestingly, and she couldn't blame it, her ride this morning had given her a healthy appetite.

'Oh, shut up!' she instructed her stomach crossly as it continued to rumble.

Footsteps could be heard coming down the passageway. 'Did you say something?' Josh taunted.

'Oh, go away!' She forgot her vow of silence in her intense hunger. 'Go away and leave me alone,' she snapped.

'I thought you said something . . .'

'Well, I didn't!'

'Okay.' The shrug could be heard in his voice, his footsteps returning to the kitchen.

Erin went over to the window, but any idea of getting out that way was soon shelved. Only the two small bottom windows opened, there was netting on the outside to keep out the insects, and they were only about nine inches square, not big enough to get out of.

Maybe reading a book would help take her mind off food? She had one in her bag, a book she had bought to read on the flight over here but had never found the time to read. It was an Agatha Christie, a Hercule Poirot story, totally absorbing, and the thought of food did get forgotten for an hour or so. But apparently the murder had taken place at a dinner, and the characters were constantly relating what they had eaten during the meal.

Erin put the book down with disgust. This wouldn't do at all! Maybe a nap? She was feeling sleepy after her read, and it would pass a little more time—until she felt it was safe to leave the bedroom without bumping into Josh. She doubted he would approve of her going off on her own again, he was already contemptuous of her behaviour.

And she had to admit she was too. His cruel words had made her aware of just how foolish she had been. He had been right to accuse her of lack of respect for herself. A little while ago she had been criticising Sharon in her mind for her lack of courage, when all the time she was being just as much of a coward. Oh, she hadn't gone as far as killing herself, but she had killed her self-respect, had given up.

And Josh had known exactly how she had been feeling. His method of bringing her to her senses might have been cruel, but it had worked. She would never be that stupid again.

Finally she slept, the lack of sleep from the night before making it impossible for her to do anything else once she lay down on the bed.

She woke with the feeling she was no longer alone. The smell of coffee seemed to confirm that feeling, and her eyes flickered open to find Josh sitting next to her prone form on the bed.

'Hi, honey,' he greeted softly.

'Hi—I mean—What are you doing in here?' she sat up indignantly, and then wished she hadn't as the movement brought her dangerously close to him. '*How* did you get in here?'

Josh grinned. 'I picked the lock. It's quite easy when you know how.'

'And you obviously know how,' she derided, swinging her legs to the floor and sitting beside him now. 'How long have you just been—sitting there?'

'Not long,' he shrugged. 'Here,' he held out the cup of coffee, 'a peace offering,' he added coaxingly.

Erin felt some of the tension finding him here start to leave her. 'Coffee?' she taunted.

'Unless you fancy beer or wine?'

'No, thanks!' she pulled a face.

'That's what I thought.' He held the cup closer to her. Erin's lips twitched at his hopeful look. 'Is it sugared?'

'Of course.'

'Then I'll take it.' She gratefully accepted the cup of steaming liquid, knowing that a hot drink would quench her thirst much better than a cold one, despite the heat of the day. Her room had grown hot and sticky while she slept, making her feel the same way.

'I think we're going to have a storm. Josh stood up to look out of the window.

'A storm?' Erin followed him, looking up at the perfectly clear blue sky. She shook her head. 'I don't think so.'

He turned to look down at her. 'Like to bet on it?'

He was too sure of himself to be wrong. 'No,' she gave a rueful smile, 'I believe you.'

'Forgiven me yet?' he asked softly.

She turned away, walking back to the bed, glad of the cup of coffee to hold on to. 'There's nothing to forgive. You merely retaliated when I hit you.'

'I wasn't talking about the slap, either of them. I certainly deserved mine, and you—well, you probably didn't deserve yours, but I thought you were going to get hysterical when you realised what I'd done.'

Her mouth twisted mockingly. 'A classic excuse.'

'Do *you* think you deserved it?'

Her head went back proudly, and she looked him straight in the eye. 'Undoubtedly.

Josh gave a half smile. 'You're letting me off lightly. I've never hit a woman before, but you made me so angry. I expected you to be sulking in here for days.'

Erin shook her head, drinking the cooling coffee. 'That isn't my way. Besides, I'm not going to be here for days.'

'Two weeks——'

'No,' she cut in firmly. 'You might as well know that I'm leaving—now. Today. I did intend just creeping off without telling you, but——'

'That isn't your way either,' he taunted. 'There's no need for you to go, Erin. I've told you I won't ask for a sexual relationship, and I won't.'

She put the empty cup down. 'Perhaps that's as well,' she said dryly. 'But that isn't the reason I'm leaving. Everything you said about me this morning was true. I'd given up, decided that if trading my body was the way to get back home then that was what I'd do.' She turned away. 'It was a disgusting—and degrading—thing to do.'

'Erin——'

'Please, let me finish. I agreed to your proposition——'

'Which I only made because I thought you were experienced,' he put in softly.

'And which I only accepted because I felt desperate. I was lost and alone, and you seemed to be offering me the hand of friendship, even if it was for a price. And—and I also—I needed——'

'I know, Erin,' Josh gathered her into his arms, stroking her hair as he held her against his chest. 'You were badly in need of someone to care for you. I knew that, and yet I've still hurt you.'

'No——'

'Yes,' he insisted, 'I have hurt you. And I didn't mean to.' He sighed, choosing his next words carefully. 'From the moment I met you I sensed your need for someone to care about you. God, you admitted as much to me. And I would have taken care of you. I would have slept with you, made love to you, given you the love and attention you needed in that way.'

She noticed he used the past tense. Could it be that he too had decided she couldn't stay here?

'Yesterday—— he continued, 'well, yesterday you took

me to the edge and then threw cold water over me, literally. It had all happened so naturally, so beautifully—or at least I thought it had.' He gave a rueful shrug. 'Then you told me about Bob being your stepfather! And I knew you were telling me more than that, were trying to let me know there'd been no one else. I just saw red. Not because of the frustration I was suffering—and God knows that was agony! I was angry because of the way you'd cheapened yourself. You asked if making you pose was a lesson like this morning—well, in a way it was. You didn't like what I did to you, hated it when I touched you——'

'You knew I hated it!' she gasped.

'Of course I knew,' he dismissed impatiently. 'But I enjoyed knowing. It showed me that you did still respect yourself. When you got up and dressed I could have kissed you!'

'I'm glad you didn't,' she swallowed hard. 'I probably would have hit you sooner.'

'But you're over all that now, aren't you?' he probed gently.

'I—I think so.'

'Then there's no reason for you to leave. We can start again, as friends. How would you like that?'

She knew that once this man had given his hand in friendship he would never take it back, but nevertheless she had reservations of it working out. 'I don't think——'

'I'll never hit you again, Erin,' Josh interrupted softly. 'I truly believe that only happened because we were both suffering from frustration. Whether you realise it or not, and being the baby you are you probably don't, you can't go that far in lovemaking without there being a build-up of sexual tension. By hitting each other I believe we've dispensed with that tension.'

Erin gave a jerky smile. 'Is making love that bad?'

'No,' Josh gave a husky laugh. 'Between the two right people it can be beautiful. Last night just wasn't the right time for us.'

She didn't like his implication that there would be a 'right' time for them. And had it been beautiful between him and Sharon? The way he talked about the other woman she had a feeling it had been.

'I'm still not sure——'

'Of course you are,' he told her briskly. 'I won't hear of your leaving. Besides,' he added with a grin, 'what would I do with two tickets to London?'

She gave a half-smile. 'There is that.'

'Good. It's settled, then. Now, how about the lunch you refused earlier?'

'I am hungry,' she admitted, 'but——'

'But nothing,' he dismissed. 'Bacon and eggs coming up!'

'Josh.'

The firmness of her tone arrested him in the doorway. 'Yes?' he asked warily.

'I won't pose for the painting, not even if it was going to be called *Innocence*.'

He nodded acknowledgement. 'It's a deal.'

Her eyes narrowed at his easy acceptance. He might have set out to humiliate her this morning, but he had been serious about the painting, she was sure of that. 'Josh?' she questioned suspiciously, even more so as he gave her a look of feigned innocence. 'What are you up to?' she asked slowly.

'Nothing.'

'Josh!'

'Well . . . it just so happens that I have total recall,' he grinned before leaving the room, once again starting that tuneless whistle.

She ran to the door, at once wishing she hadn't as her

stiff legs and thighs protested at such treatment. 'Josh!' she called in exasperation.

'Mm?' He turned, a mischievous glitter to his eyes.

'Oh, nothing! Except—except that isn't fair,' she told him crossly. 'You really can remember everything?' she frowned, blushing profusely.

'Everything,' he laughed at her discomfort. 'In Technicolor.'

'Oh.'

'It's helpful in my profession.'

'I suppose so,' she muttered.

'One meal coming up,' he teased.

'Shouldn't I be doing that?' she offered grudgingly, not liking the idea of Josh being able to recall her nakedness, vividly, every time he wanted to. Not that she had forgotten the perfection of his body either, the tanned broadness of his shoulders, tapered waist, and powerful thighs, his legs long and muscular.

He shrugged. 'Part of my peace offering.'

'Okay,' she accepted. 'I just want to get changed.'

'You look fine as you are.'

'I'm sticky,' she insisted.

'Suit yourself,' he shrugged.

Their relationship had changed already, she could tell that. Before Josh's attitude had been slightly possessive, even dictatorial; now he treated her as an equal, as someone whose opinions and thoughts were important enough to listen to. It was a good feeling.

Even though she had been looking forward to her meal, was feeling hungry, she still couldn't eat all of it. 'It was lovely,' she assured Josh.

He was frowning darkly. 'It's your first meal of the day, you should have eaten more than that.' He cleaned her plate and put it into the dishwasher.

'I told you——'

'That you never eat much,' he finished grimly. 'I don't like it, Erin. I don't like it at all.'

'I can't help it——'

'I know you can't. Which makes it all the more worrying.'

She gave an impatient sigh. 'You aren't really serious about this anorexia nervosa?'

'I am,' he nodded curtly. 'If you haven't started eating normally before the end of this two weeks I'm taking you to a doctor.'

'I——'

'It's no good arguing, Erin,' he told her in a firm voice. 'I'll do it, whether you want it or not.'

She could see that he would too. She felt a warm glow at his concern, and it was a genuine concern. But she had gone so long now with only small meals, or no meal at all, that it was bound to take time to build up a normal appetite again.

'I'm really all right, Josh,' she assured him as he still frowned.

'You're going to be,' he nodded. 'It isn't too late for you. You're thin, but not like——' he broke off, turning away. 'Let's go outside, you can help me do the garden.'

'Not like . . .?' Erin prompted, sensing some deep hurt.

He drew in a deep breath, looking at her with pained eyes. 'I knew someone who had that disease—and it is a disease, a sickness like everything else in this damned fashion-conscious, body-conscious world!' His tone was savage. 'Anorexia nervosa is a disease caused by society, and it *kills*!'

'Josh——'

He swung away from her. 'Let's go outside,' he rasped.

Erin followed him slowly, Sheba at his heels. Josh's anger, his pain, were so strong, so deep-felt, that she knew with sudden clarity that the sufferer from anorexia nervosa that he was so impassioned about was Sharon; it had to be Sharon. That pretty dark-haired girl in the photograph at Dave's, and the painting in Josh's studio, had killed herself because of the diet disease.

'Josh!' She had followed him out to the garage where he seemed to be in the process of starting a small tractor. 'What on earth is that?' she asked, momentarily side-tracked.

'A lawnmower.' He gave a tight smile.

'Lazy!' she shook her head.

'So would you be if it took you a week to cut the lawn with an ordinary hand-mower. I almost broke my back the only time I tried that.'

'Josh,' she put a hand on his arm, 'tell me about Sharon.'

'Sharon?' He looked startled. 'But——'

'Tell me about her, please.'

'Maybe I should at that,' he rasped. 'Maybe shock treatment is what you need.'

She didn't contradict him, but let him talk, listening in silence as he spoke of the woman he had loved.

'She was twenty-three, Erin, just twenty-three,' he said in a harsh voice. 'Beautiful to look at, and so full of life. Even as a child——'

'As a child?' Erin frowned her puzzlement.

He nodded. 'She was a beautiful baby. Everybody loved her. And my mama was so proud of her——'

'*Your* mother? Sharon was your *sister*?' she realised won-deringly.

'Well, of course—Hey,' he gave her a searching look, 'what did you think she was? You thought—you thought—My God, she was going to marry Dave!'

'I know, but I——'

'You thought I wasn't averse to taking my best friend's fiancée from him.' Josh's mouth twisted with distaste.

'That's some opinion you have of me, lady!'

'Oh, Josh, I didn't mean——'

'I know exactly what you meant, Erin,' he said disgustedly, 'and I'm not flattered.'

She gave a sigh of exasperation. 'No one explained your relationship to Sharon. How was I supposed to know you were her brother?'

'You could have asked, damn you!'

That Josh was furious with her she had no doubt, that he had reason to be she wasn't so sure. She wasn't psychic, she couldn't possibly have known that Sharon was his sister. And she had no idea why it made her feel good to know that. Maybe it was because she felt relieved to know Josh hadn't betrayed his friend after all. Yes, that had to be the reason she suddenly felt so lighthearted.

'And you could have told me, damn you!' she snapped back at him, holding her breath as she waited for his reaction.

He gave her an impatient look. 'I—You—Oh hell!' He scowled at her.

She quirked a hopeful eyebrow at him, sensing a lessening of his anger. 'Hell, what?'

'Just hell.' He pulled a face, shrugging his resignation. 'Okay, so no one told you I was Sharon's brother. And you didn't ask.'

'I didn't think it was any of my business,' she dared to add.

'It wasn't, it still isn't. Except that I don't take other people's girls from them, especially my best friend.'

'I thought you loved her. After all, we can't choose who we love.'

'Too true.' His mouth twisted mockingly. 'If we could we would all end up with Mr and Miss Right.'

'The world might be less complicated.'

'And more boring,' Josh added dryly.

'Maybe,' she conceded. 'I—Do you want to tell me about Sharon, or would you rather not?'

'I think I'd better. I went to school with Dave, it was through me that the two of them met. Sharon fell in love with him when she was sixteen years old, and I think he felt the same way. But she was still a kid, whereas he was already twenty-five. He spoke to my mother and father about his feelings, told them he wanted to marry her, and they told him they wanted her to finish her education, college, the whole bit. I suppose they thought they were doing the right thing at the time.'

'But you don't think so,' Erin put in softly.

'Hell, I couldn't wait seven years to marry the girl I loved! But I guess Dave's made of sterner stuff than me. He agreed with them, agreed to keep his feelings to himself until Sharon was older.' He shrugged. 'Sharon finished school, then she went on to college, as planned.'

'And when she came home Dave asked her to marry him.' It sounded a romantic story, which made it all the stranger that Sharon had taken her own life.

'Yes,' Josh confirmed. 'Except that Sharon already had this dieting sickness. I think she wanted Dave to be interested in her, didn't know that he already loved her, and she thought that by being slimmer she would get his attention. None of us knew about it, we just put the loss of weight down to working too hard. Then when Dave asked her to marry him she seemed to put some of the weight back on. Everything seemed okay, until she decided she had to be thinner for her wedding dress. Oh, she seemed happy enough, very much in love, looking forward to the wedding, and none of us guessed what was really wrong with her.' His voice broke emotionally. 'She didn't realise she was sick, that this obsessive dieting——'

'Don't tell me any more if you'd rather not,' Erin gently touched his arm. 'I think I can guess the rest.'

'Yes,' he sighed heavily, 'I suppose you can. My mother and father still haven't got over the shock. And you've seen Dave. I guess we all blame ourselves for not realising——'

'But you couldn't have known,' she protested. 'They hide it so well.'

'Yes. But it doesn't make it any easier to bear, knowing that she took her own life because she was so damned scared of getting fat.'

'I don't have that, Josh,' she assured him softly. 'Really, I don't. I've just been too tired to eat. You'll see, after two weeks of eating properly I'll be back to my normal chubby self.'

'If you say so. But I'm still going to be keeping a close watch on you.'

Erin could understand his concern. The dieting disease was something doctors had only recently accepted as an actual disease, something that needed to be treated like any other sickness. There had been several television programmes on the subject in England just before she left, and the tragedy of it was that these people just couldn't help themselves, even though a lot of them wanted to.

'Hey, are we going to do this gardening or not?' She attempted lightness, promising herself that she would make sure she ate in future if only to reassure Josh.

'We are,' he picked up her mood. 'You pull out the weeds and I'll cut the lawn.'

She frowned. 'I think I came out worse in that deal.'

Josh shook his head. 'Sheba is going to help you. She likes to weed. Well, actually, she likes to dig holes, but she usually gets rid of a few weeds at the same time.'

She was getting used to the huge dog, although she was still wary of her. The two of them did the weeding while Josh drove up and down on the smooth lawn, his thoughts far away, from the look on his face.

Erin hadn't meant to bring back unhappy memories for him, and so for the rest of the day she set out to be entertaining, knowing she had succeeded in putting Sharon from his mind as they spent a quiet evening together.

Josh looked at her closely. 'You look tired, why don't you go to bed?'

The mention of being tired made her yawn, a reflex action. 'I think I might just do that. Working for Mike was hard work, but today has been rather hectic too. What are you smiling about?' she asked suspiciously as he grinned.

'How English you sound. It's really rather attractive,' he mimicked her accent.

Erin gave him a look of disgust. 'I hate to be teased— and you seem to do little else.'

'Sorry,' but he didn't look in the least repentant. 'But I can't help it if I find your English accent sexy.'

She blushed anew, and stood up. 'I'm going to bed!' His mocking laughter followed her out of the room.

Josh really was impossible! She never knew from one moment to the next what he was going to say—and it was usually outrageous!

She almost collapsed into bed when she reached her room, not willing to admit it, but her body seemed to have stiffened up from her horse ride and the gardening. She must be terribly out of condition for her legs and back to ache like this.

But it was the tender skin on her inner thighs that felt the worst. They felt deeply bruised, although they didn't look it, and the skin seemed to be burning. She had been in agony for the last hour or so, but she hadn't been willing to admit her discomfort to Josh.

She felt so sore it was impossible to sleep, so she moved restlessly about in the bed, wondering what she could possibly put on her legs to soothe away the burning pain.

Josh had gone to his bedroom hours ago, she had heard

him use his shower before climbing into bed. And still she moved about restlessly, wishing she could sleep but knowing it was impossible in the circumstances.

Suddenly the bedroom door opened, and Josh stood there, his only clothing a dark towelling robe. 'What's wrong?' he asked sharply.

'I—er—Why, nothing,' she lied. 'I—I'm just a bit restless, that's all.'

'A bit!' he scorned. 'You're moving about so much you're making it impossible for me to sleep too.'

'I'm sorry,' she muttered, clutching the bedclothes to her.

'What's wrong with you?' he repeated impatiently.

'I—I'm uncomfortable,' she evaded, her cheeks fiery red.

'The bed——'

'No, not the bed,' she snapped resentfully.

'Then what—Ah,' Josh began to smile, the smile turning to laughter, open laughter that mocked her blushes. 'Painful, is it?' he taunted when he could contain his amusement long enough to speak.

'Yes, it is—if you must know!' She turned away.

'Oh, I think I must, Erin,' the amusement was still in his voice. 'Have you put anything on it?'

'Like what?' she snapped again, glaring at him.

'In that case, I guess you haven't. I'll go and get you some cream. I might even offer to put it on for you,' came his parting taunt.

Like hell he would!

CHAPTER SEVEN

SHE was in the middle of struggling out of bed when Josh came back into the room, her stiffened limbs making it impossible for her to move any faster.

He quirked a mocking eyebrow. 'Going somewhere?'

'I—Just out of bed.' She swung her legs to the floor to sit on the side of the bed. 'Is that the cream?' she held out her hand for it.

'I believe I offered to put it on for you?'

'No, thank you.' She still held out her hand for the tube of cream he had in his hand.

'No?'

'No!'

'Shame,' he shrugged resignedly. 'Did you have another bath?'

'I didn't have the strength,' she admitted ruefully. 'I was going to have a shower, but I couldn't work out how the shower in the bathroom works.'

'You could have used mine.'

She remembered what had happened the last time she did that. 'No . . .'

Josh obviously remembered too, and his eyes darkened in colour. Of course he remembered, hadn't he said he had total recall!

'Maybe not,' he agreed tersely. 'Anyway, you need a good long soak in the bath. Go and have one now, before you put the cream on.'

'I'll disturb you——'

'No,' he shook his head, 'I'm going up to my studio.'

'Now?' she gasped, knowing it was after one o'clock in the morning.

'Now,' he nodded. 'I have this sudden urge to paint. Actually, the urge is much more basic,' he added derisively. 'But for the sake of friendship, and my peace of mind, I think it would be best if I exerted my energy on painting you, not making love to you.'

Erin's cheeks were scarlet by this time. 'I—You still intend painting me?'

'With your permission, yes.'

'Nude?'

'Yes.'

'I see,' she bit her lip. 'I can't stop you . . .'

'Do you want to?' His voice had deepened huskily.

Erin looked at him as if mesmerised, watched as he came closer and closer, felt the bed dip as he sat down next to her, felt the warmth of his arm as it came about her waist, his hand resting just below the curve of her breast.

'Do you want to stop me, Erin?' he breathed softly, his face only inches from hers now.

She should say yes, she had to say yes—didn't she? But did she? Yes, she did! Josh had given her a lesson in self-respect today, and she couldn't go against that.

She moved away from him. 'I think I'll take up your suggestion and have a bath. The way I feel right now I need to soak every inch of me.'

Josh stood up. 'I'll be up in the studio if you should need me,' he told her abruptly. He stopped at the door. 'Do I have your permission to paint you?'

She pretended concentration on collecting her toiletries together so that she didn't have to look at him. 'Yes.'

Her tension left her in a sigh as he softly closed the door as he left. Josh had had a very thin control over his emotions just now, one word or movement of encouragement from her and he would have been making love to her right now. So much for friendship! Someone had once said it was impossible to have true friendship between a man and a woman. She was beginning to think they were right!

Josh's mood the next day was explosive. Erin was exposed to his temper as soon as he came into the kitchen the next morning.

'No breakfast for me,' he snapped, pouring himself some black coffee before sitting down at the breakfast bar.

She turned from the stove. 'But I've cooked it now.' She had got up early to make sure she was ready to cook Josh's breakfast as soon as she heard him moving about his bedroom. She hadn't heard what time he had gone to bed; the bath and soothing cream had done the trick, so much so that she had fallen asleep as soon as she got back into bed. Whatever time Josh had got to bed it hadn't agreed with him.

'I said I'm not hungry.' He stood up forcefully, putting his empty cup down on the side.

'But——'

'Did you sleep last night?' he cut in abruptly.

'Yes, thank you. Did you?'

'Once the storm had passed, yes.'

'Storm?' she blinked. 'What storm?'

'The one we had in the night,' he said dryly.

'But I didn't hear any storm.'

'No, you wouldn't have heard it, it was an electric storm.'

'Like the one you painted,' Erin said excitedly. She remembered the painting well, the dark sky suddenly alight with pink light, the moment captured for all time beneath Josh's expert talent.

He didn't return her smile. 'Yes.'

She shook her head regretfully. 'I missed it.'

His mouth twisted. 'Don't worry, there'll be others. We

get a lot of those type of storms, and they aren't always that quiet. Usually we get loud thunder too, and occasionally rain.' He moved to the door, picking up his hat on the way.

'Where are you going?' asked Erin.

'For a ride.' His tone wasn't encouraging.

She ran her hands nervously down her thighs, not knowing Josh in this unapproachable mood. 'Can I come?'

He gave her a derisive glance. 'I doubt that would be a good idea. How are you feeling today?'

'Better,' she blushed. 'And I'd like to come with you—really.'

He shrugged. 'Please yourself.'

That seemed to be his attitude towards her over the next few days. She could do what she wanted, as long as she didn't get in his way. And she didn't do that; she made herself as unobtrusive as possible, being used to doing that around Bob. After all, Josh was the artist, and as such he was entitled to his artistic temperament.

And she wasn't the only one he shut out. Sheba seemed to spend a lot of her time sitting at the bottom of the stairs waiting for her master to come out of his studio.

Josh made no effort to tell Erin how he was progressing with the painting of her, although he seemed to spend every waking minute up in his studio, hardly touching the meals she prepared for him. She knew she wasn't the best cook in the world, but she wasn't the worst either, so it couldn't be her cooking that was putting him off.

The only time Josh seemed to truly relax was during their early morning rides together. Her own relationship with Blaize reaching an understanding—she didn't tell him where to go as long as he didn't wander too far from Josh and the stallion! She would never make a horse-woman, but she enjoyed it enough to join in the daily ride.

And if she hadn't, she wouldn't have spent any time with Josh at all.

She jumped nervously as the studio door slammed shut, heard the sound of pounding feet coming down the stairs. She was sitting in the lounge quietly reading a book, but she looked up curiously as Josh reached the bottom of the stairs.

'Is there anything wrong?' she asked anxiously as he glowered down at her.

'Not a damn thing.' His mouth twisted derisively.

Something was definitely wrong, she could clearly see that. Josh looked as if he had been pulling his hair out, small tufts of it stood on end, and his expression was harassed.

Erin bit her lip. 'How's your work going?'

It seemed she had said the one thing to make him look even grimmer. 'It isn't,' he snapped.

'Oh.'

'Aren't you interested in *why* it isn't?' he asked tautly.

'Er—why?' Heavens, he looked ready to explode, his eyes deeply green, a cynical twist to his mouth. She couldn't understand him saying his work wasn't going well, he had been constantly up in his studio for days now.

'Because of you,' he rasped. 'Because of your damned body!'

Colour flooded her cheeks. 'I——'

'Oh, don't worry,' he scorned at her flustered manner. 'It isn't your fault. I just can't do it.'

'But you said you had total recall.' Her cheeks were still coloured a delicate pink.

'And I do. But I can't—I just—You—Oh, hell!' He dropped down beside her on the sofa, his hands coming up to cup either side of her face. 'What the hell is so elusive about you?' he muttered almost to himself.

Erin blinked dazedly. 'Elusive? Me?'

'Yes,' he said savagely. 'You're driving me insane,' he moaned, his lips taking possession of hers.

Erin responded without reserve, her arms going up about his neck as the book she had been reading fell slowly to the ground, forgotten by both of them.

Josh kissed her with a hunger that made her gasp, caressing her restlessly from breast to thigh, lingering on the latter before moving his hand to cup and hold her breast. She pressed herself against him as excitement thrilled through her body, touching the broadness of his back with questing fingers, knowing he was as aroused as she was.

Tension, and—dared she admit it, frustration, made her response explosive, at once feeling on fire for Josh, sensing that he felt the same way. She shuddered with pleasure as his hand moved below her sun-top, caressing her heated body, seeking the erect flesh beneath her bra, touching the tautness of her nipple almost wonderingly.

'Oh, Erin,' he kissed her throat with probing lips and tongue, 'I'm going out of my mind thinking about you. Day and night, I can't get you out of my head.'

She felt the same way; she had been aware of a growing attraction to him the last few days, an attraction that had now reached fever pitch.

But suddenly he was pushing her away from him, moving back with a shake of his head. 'Just what the hell am I doing to you?' once again he spoke to himself. 'I'm sorry, Erin,' he said stiltedly, standing up, 'I didn't mean for that to happen.'

'Josh——'

'Come on, Sheba,' he turned to the dog, opening the door. 'Don't get me any dinner, Erin,' he told her abruptly. 'I won't be back in time.'

She quickly stood up, straightening her top. 'You're going out?'

He nodded. 'I think I should. Don't you?' he asked tautly.

'I—I—Yes, I suppose so.' She looked down at her hands, wishing she had the nerve to ask him to stay. But somehow she had disappointed him, her inexperience making him turn away from her. 'But you'll be back before it gets dark?' The quiver in her voice showed her nervousness.

'Yes, I'll be back,' he nodded abruptly. 'And, Erin— that was A-plus.' He closed the door quietly as he left.

A-plus . . .! But—She ran to the door. 'Josh——' She was just in time to see the pick-up disappearing down the driveway, Sheba standing regally in the back.

A-plus! Josh had given her A-plus. Then why had he stopped when he did! Why—What on earth was she saying? If he hadn't stopped they would be lovers now. Suddenly it no longer bothered her. Oh, not because of any lack of self-respect, as Josh said, she was 'over that' now. But love had entered her life, when she least expected it, and wasn't even sure she wanted it. She mistrusted all men, didn't want them in her life, and yet Josh was different. He had to be—she loved him.

She wasn't even sure when it had happened, only that she had been longing for him to kiss her the last four days, had been hurt by his coldness, had tried in every way she knew how to please him, and had received only scowls for her trouble. But he had said he had been thinking of her day and night too, that she was driving him insane. She hugged the memory of that to herself. Surely that meant he cared for her too?

There wasn't any sign that he did when he got back two hours later, although his bad mood seemed to have evaporated.

'Like a beer?' he asked on his way to the kitchen.

'Er—no, thanks.' She had been wary of his mood, but he seemed quite cheerful, whistling to himself as he moved about the kitchen. 'Where have you been?' she asked softly when he joined her in the lounge.

'To Jim and Martha's.'

'Oh.' She couldn't hide her disappointment. She liked the bungalow, enjoyed its peace and quiet, but she would have enjoyed seeing the other couple again. It would have been nice to talk to Martha. Josh left her on her own so much that it would just have been nice to talk to *someone*. 'How are they?'

'Fine. I know,' he gave a deep sigh, 'I should have taken you with me.' He shrugged. 'I wasn't thinking straight when I left here.'

'No . . . About earlier——'

'I did it again, didn't I?' he gave a rueful shrug. 'I can't seem to keep my hands off you. Pathetic, isn't it?'

'Pathetic . . .?'

'Yes.' He stood up. 'I'm ashamed of myself.'

'You are?' Erin frowned her puzzlement, any chance of being able to tell him she loved him disappearing with each word he said.

'Yes. I'm a man, with a man's normal appetites, including sex. And you must be sick as hell of my attempts to get you into bed with me.'

'Josh——'

'Don't blame me too much, Erin. You're an attractive girl, and you already know I'd like to take you to bed. But it isn't fair to keep subjecting you to my——'

'Sexual harassment,' she put in bitterly, realising that to him that was all it was. He was attracted to her, wanted to make love to her, but emotions such as love didn't enter into that want, that need. Once again she felt her feelings become numb, the love and trust she had started to feel towards this man pushed to the back of her subconscious.

'Yes,' he bit out tautly, not looking at her. 'But it won't happen again.'

'It won't?' she said dully.

'Definitely not,' he said briskly. 'Now I'm going upstairs to work. Oh, by the way, we're going to Martha and Jim's for dinner on Saturday.'

'We are?' she asked eagerly.

'Yes,' Josh grimaced. 'Martha talked me into making a definite promise. What the hell, I can't work anyway.' He threw some of the beer to the back of his throat, swallowing deeply.

'I'm sorry,' she muttered.

'It isn't your fault. Although I must admit this has never happened to me before.'

'You've never painted a nude before—you said so.'

'I did in college, and I certainly never had this trouble with it. Maybe I'm going about it all wrong,' he said thoughtfully. 'Yes,' his face lit up with excitement. 'Yes, that's it!' He put down the empty beer can. 'I'm not doing this logically.'

'A question of lust spoiling your art,' Erin derided, hurt that she was only a body to him.

'Something like that,' he nodded. 'You sound pleased about going out on Saturday.' His eyes were narrowed. 'Bored with my company already?'

She hadn't had enough of it to be bored! 'I——'

'We have over a week to go,' he derided. 'Think you'll be able to stand it?'

'Of course,' she flushed. 'You're deliberately mis-understanding me. It will just be nice to see another woman, to talk. You wouldn't understand——'

'Oh, but I do. I live a strange life, Erin. In the winter I hardly see anyone, and in the summer I tour the world with my paintings. It's a strange life, but I like it. But I doubt many other people would, especially a woman. Why do you think I've never asked a woman to share my life?'

'I just thought you'd never met the woman you wanted

to share your life with,' she mocked.

His mouth twisted. 'As it happens, I haven't. But even if I had I'd hesitate about asking her to share this. Being the wife of an artist may appear glamorous, but I can assure you, being *my* wife would be very unglamorous. Martha and Jim, and possibly Dave, are the only people I see all winter. No woman in her right mind would be able to stand that sort of solitude.'

'Women in love aren't usually in their right mind,' she derided.

Josh laughed. 'I never thought of that! Thanks, Erin.'

'You're welcome,' she mumbled as he once again left her.

It seemed she had now put marriage in the mind of the man she loved—marriage to some other woman!

Martha and Jim were just as friendly as she remembered, which was perhaps as well, with Josh glowering at them all. His good mood of three nights ago had evaporated by the next morning, and she had once again been ignored, or snapped at.

It was obvious that once again the painting wasn't going well, and she made a tentative offer to sit for him again, fully clothed, of course. Josh's reply had been blistering in the extreme, and she hadn't offered again.

This visit to Martha and Jim had come as a welcome break, although Josh didn't seem to see it the same way, resenting losing the time. When Erin had pointed out that he hadn't been working very well anyway, his reply had been unrepeatable.

Still, he did have some semblance of manners in front of the other couple, had even eaten the delicious meal Martha had prepared for them, something Erin hadn't been able to get him to do all week.

'Josh tells us you've learnt to ride,' Martha said conversationally, perched on the edge of her husband's armchair. Their marriage was obviously a close one.

Erin shot Josh a sharp look, but he didn't even seem to be listening to the conversation, staring sightlessly into space. 'Yes.' She still remembered her embarrassed pain after that first ride.

Martha nodded. 'It's a definite asset out here.'

She pulled a face. 'But not much of one in London.'

'No, I suppose not,' the other woman smiled. 'You're going back for a visit, are you?'

'I——'

'Erin is coming with me next week.' It seemed Josh was listening to the conversation after all. 'Aren't you, honey?'

It was the first show of warmth she had received from him in days, and to her shame her heart leapt with pleasure. 'Yes,' she smiled shyly at him.

'That will be nice for you,' Martha smiled. 'I wonder if you'll be as glad to get back here as Josh usually is.'

'Oh, but I——'

'Home is where the heart is,' Josh remarked lazily, his arm dropping in casual possession about her shoulders. 'Isn't that so, sweetheart?'

She could see the other couple looking on approvingly, and wondered at Josh's sudden change towards her. 'I—er—yes,' she agreed awkwardly.

'How's Sabre now?' he turned to ask Jim, his black mood evaporating.

'Better. Like to come out and see her?' the other man offered.

'Oh, not now, Jim!' his wife protested. 'I thought we could all sit here and have a chat.'

'You two girls have a chat,' Josh drawled. 'I know that's what you're dying to do anyway. But don't try and get too many of my secrets out of Erin, Martha,' he mocked. 'She's a little on the shy side.'

Hot colour blazed in Erin's cheeks. Josh was deliberately giving his friends the impression that their own relationship was much closer than it actually was. Maybe it was a pride-saver, but she didn't like it.

'It isn't a question of being shy,' she returned coolly. 'As I don't know any of your secrets I can hardly tell them to Martha.'

He grinned, obviously enjoying her embarrassment. 'In that case you won't be telling Martha about my birthmark, or the scar at the top of my thigh that I got playing football at college.'

If anything her colour deepened. Both of the distinguishing marks were known to her—and the guilt in her face showed that they were. Damn him! She gave him a rebellious look. 'Just as you won't mention——'

'Your appendix scar,' he finished in a slow drawl. 'No, I won't mention it,' he taunted, kissing her lightly on the nose before standing up. 'So it's agreed we'll keep those things to ourselves.'

'Yes,' she said tautly, not even realising he had seen the small scar. But of course, he would have seen every inch of her as she posed for him.

Martha spluttered with laughter as soon as the two women were alone. 'You mustn't mind Josh,' she chuckled. 'I've known him all my life, and he can still surprise me.'

'He—I——'

'He's impossible,' Martha finished for her. 'I know. But he's the best friend Jim and I ever had.'

Erin appreciated that he was a loyal friend, but did he have to embarrass her like that? Was he so intent on showing what a stud he was that he had to lie about it?

'More coffee?' Martha offered at her continued silence.

'Oh—er—yes, please.' She followed the other girl out to the kitchen. 'That was a really lovely meal you cooked us.' She had enjoyed the barbecued chicken and baked potato immensely, trying sour cream on the latter, and finding she liked it. Martha had also made an apple pie, not the insipid type usually found in England; the apples were cooked in a brown syrup that gave them a lovely flavour.

'Thank you,' Martha accepted shyly. 'Josh told us he's painting you.' She handed the refilled cup to Erin.

'He did?' Erin licked her lips nervously, wondering if he had told them it was a nude.

'Mm. How's it going?'

'All right—I think.' How could she tell the other girl that Josh hadn't so much as let her step into the studio since the one and only time she had sat for him.

Martha nodded, not seeming surprised by her lack of knowledge about the painting. 'He's a bit protective about his work.'

'Yes,' she agreed in a relieved voice.

'I hope he shows it to us before you go to England, I'd really like to see it. Does it have a title? He usually gives them a name.'

After the way Josh had been acting minutes earlier, his familiarity, how could she tell Martha it was called *Innocence*? Although it certainly didn't sound as if Josh had done more than mention he was painting her; Martha did not seem to know it was a nude. 'I don't think so,' she evaded. 'He—He's been so—intense—so erratic in his moods that——'

'*Josh* has?' Martha's eyes were wide. 'That doesn't sound like Josh. He's usually very even-tempered.'

Erin had thought so too at first, but his behaviour lately had been volcanic—and she was never quite sure when he was going to erupt!

'I think he's been working too hard,' she excused. 'And this last painting is just extra work for him.'

'But a labour of love, surely? No, don't answer,' Martha sighed. 'It's none of my business. I don't know why I said it. Josh would be furious if he knew—he hates people to be curious about his private life.'

Erin wasn't sure she liked being under the heading of Josh's 'private life', but at least it saved her further embarrassing questions. 'Did you manage to persuade Jim to take you to England yet?' She changed the subject before Martha's curiosity overcame her good manners.

'Not yet,' Martha smiled. 'But I'm still working on it. I think I'll succeed.'

'Maybe you could come and see me while you're there,' Erin suggested eagerly. She really liked the other girl and would enjoy seeing her again. Besides, Martha would then be able to tell her how Josh was.

Martha looked puzzled. 'Oh, but surely you and Josh——'

'Erin and I what?' Josh drawled as he came into the kitchen, his arm once again going about Erin's shoulders as he held her to his side.

'I was just inviting Martha to visit me if she comes to England next year,' Erin told him firmly, challenge in her bright blue eyes.

'Impossible, sweetheart,' he said lazily, the sharpness of his gaze belying the relaxation of his mood. 'Jim's just asked me to keep an eye on the ranch for him while they're away—but don't tell him I told you, puss,' he tapped his cousin warningly on the nose. 'So we won't be able to be in England with them too.' He looked back at her with equal challenge.

'But——'

'We have to leave now, honey,' he cut in softly. 'I need to get back to work, and there's a storm coming up.'

'Another one?' Erin groaned her dismay, forgetting for the moment his implication that she would still be in Canada with him next year. Almost every day brought one of the electric storms. The vast changes in the temperature were blamed for these fierce storms, and Erin had found she didn't like them, finding their intensity frightening, hating the loud thunder that accompanied the lightning; the whole house seemed to shake sometimes.

Josh nodded. 'And I think this one is going to be the worst one yet.'

If Josh said so then she knew it to be a fact, he seemed to have a sixth sense about the storms. 'Then we should be going,' she agreed hastily. She certainly didn't want to get caught in the thunder and lightning on the drive home.

'Don't give us that,' Jim said laughingly. 'We know you just want to get home in time to watch the football on television,' he teased his friend.

Josh's mouth quirked with humour. 'How well you know me,' he drawled.

Jim gave him a steady look, suddenly serious as he glanced at Erin. 'I thought I did, buddy. I thought I did.'

Josh met his friend's gaze unflinchingly. 'Don't be deceived by impressions, Jim,' he advised softly.

Erin looked away. The two men's conversation might not be completely out in the open, but its meaning was clear. Jim couldn't understand Josh's interest in her. She must obviously be different from the usual type Josh went for, and Josh was giving the other man the impression that there was more to her than met the eye.

'Why did you do that?' She turned on him angrily on the drive home.

'What?' His curtness was back with a vengeance.

'You deliberately let them think—*made* them think, that you and I sleep together!' she glared at him.

'Rubbish.'

'You did! You——'

'I don't want to talk about it, Erin.'

'Well, that's too bad, because *I* do!' Her voice rose in her anger. 'What's the matter, Josh? Is the Hawke ego so inflated that you had to let your friends think we were sleeping together even though we aren't?'

His eyes were like green pebbles as he looked at her coldly. 'The "Hawke ego" isn't inflated at all—at least, not where you're concerned. I let Martha and Jim go on thinking what they did because when we saw them last week it was obvious that we *were* going to sleep together. Did it occur to you that it would have been more embarrassing, caused more speculation, if we'd continued to act as if we hate each other?'

Hate each other? Her anger evaporated into numbed silence. She didn't hate Josh, far from it, but it appeared Josh hated her.

He switched on the football match once they got home, putting several cans of beer next to his chair as he waited for the match to start, an aura of silence surrounding him that he didn't encourage her to break.

Not that she wanted to; she was too miserable to want to enter into a conversation herself. She had entered into this situation sick of herself and everyone else, but now she felt even sicker. She, Erin Richards, the girl who had sworn that no man would ever hurt her again, had fallen in love with a man who cared nothing for her, a man who now found it difficult to even be polite to her, not even attempting to be so when they were alone.

Suddenly he stood up, turning to look down at her. 'I'm going up to the studio,' he told her abruptly.

'I—Okay,' she shrugged. 'But I thought you were watching the football.'

'It isn't what it used to be.'

She couldn't say she liked it. She had been expecting the English version of the game, belatedly remembering that was called soccer over here, the football being shown on the television being more like English rugby. And she didn't like that either. The object of both games seemed, to her, to be to hurt your opponent, not to score points.

'Then I might as well go to bed,' she said resignedly.

Josh scowled. 'Don't go on my account. If you don't like the football then switch to another channel.'

'No,' she shook her head. 'I—I'm feeling rather tired. Maybe I'll sleep through the storm,' she said hopefully.

'I doubt it,' he gave a rueful smile. 'I can hear the rumbling of the thunder already.'

So could she, which was why she would rather try and sleep through it. 'Can Sheba come in?' she asked.

He quirked an eyebrow. 'Do you want her to?'

'Yes.'

'Then let her in. You're spoiling her, you know,' he sighed. 'Once you're gone she'll still expect to come in at night.'

Erin had brought the dog into the house for company the last few evenings, but she hadn't realised Josh had known about it, only bringing Sheba in once he had gone up to his studio. 'She can guard as well from the inside as she can the outside,' she defended; she and the dog had become quite good friends in Josh's absence. The poor dog craved his love as badly as she did! 'I'll let her out if she hears anything.'

'Okay,' he shrugged. 'I'll see you in the morning. Are you riding tomorrow?'

'Yes,' she replied stubbornly. Josh asked her the same question every night, hoping, she felt sure, that she would refuse. But she wouldn't. She loved the closeness of their early morning rides together, and was unwilling to give them up. They rarely spoke during these rides, but the silence wasn't strained as it was the rest of the day, but more companionable. Actually, the conversation they were having now was the longest they had had for a long time.

'Seven o'clock,' Josh murmured needlessly before leaving her.

Erin stared dejectedly at the padded men moving about the football pitch, wishing she could take the knocks life kept giving her as easily as they took the tackles of the other players.

A flash of lightning that lit up the whole house brought her out of her reverie, lighting up the gloom of the room brighter than any electric light. She hastily stood up and switched off the television, moving to let Sheba into the house. The dog licked her hand, sitting down at her feet.

'I know, girl,' she bent down to absently pat the dog's head. 'It's horrible, isn't it?' Sheba didn't seem particularly bothered by the storms they had been having, but it helped to be able to talk to someone. No doubt if Josh had known the full extent of her fear he would have stayed with her himself, but it wasn't his forced company she wanted.

Even though she had pulled the curtains she could still see the lightning as she lay in bed, the sky seeming to go pink for several long seconds before it was all darkness again. And then the thunder started, as Josh had predicted, the worst yet, the crash seeming to be overhead as the whole house trembled on its foundations.

Erin buried her head under the bedclothes, wishing the storm would stop, but knowing from experience that it would go on for hours. She wasn't usually nervous of storms, but she had never seen such lightning in England. And they were aptly named 'electric storms'; you could almost see the air crackle.

She couldn't stand it any longer! Josh might not like her, and he might not want her in his studio, but she couldn't be on her own a moment longer.

She pulled her robe on over her serviceable pyjamas, padding her way out of the bedroom and up to the studio. She hesitated outside the door, a vicious crack of thunder overhead making her knock hastily on the door before entering. Josh had his back towards her, and didn't seem aware of her presence, staring at the blank canvas in front of him.

For several moments Erin forgot all about the storm, aware only of that blank canvas. Josh had been up here for hours without end, long into the night most of the time, and all he had to show for it was a blank canvas!

'Josh . . .'

He turned as if in a daze. 'Erin?'

'I—The storm,' she shrugged her awkwardness. 'I couldn't sleep.'

He slowly stood up, pale beneath his tanned skin. 'You shouldn't have come up here.'

She swallowed hard, not understanding his mood at all. 'I—I was frightened. I thought perhaps I could just—sit up here with you?'

'No,' Josh shook his head.

'No . . ?'

'I don't think so.' He still spoke in that strange voice.

'Of course, if you don't want me here,' she blinked back her tears, 'I'll go back to my room.'

'I didn't say that. You——'

'Josh!' she screamed as the lights suddenly went out, the darkness absolute. 'Josh, where are you?' she didn't attempt to hide her panic. 'Josh!' She groped blindly in the blackness.

'It's all right, honey,' he murmured close to her ear, his arms coming about her waist from behind. 'I've got you.'

'Oh, Josh,' she sobbed, turning into his body, her arms going up about his neck. 'Hold me, Josh. Hold me!'

'I have to,' his voice was ragged. 'Oh God, Erin, I have to make love to you!' and his mouth came down firmly on hers.

CHAPTER EIGHT

THE hunger of days was dammed up inside her, all of it coming out as she eagerly returned that kiss, her hands clinging to his shoulders as she arched against him.

'Erin, Erin,' Josh murmured between heated kisses, his hands fevered on her back, resting possessively on her hips to pull her into him, his thighs hard and demanding. 'Erin, let me love you,' he groaned.

'Yes,' she breathed huskily, unbuttoning his shirt down to his navel, eagerly touching the hard flesh beneath.

'God, I wish I could see your face!'

She took one of his hands and placed it against her lips, kissing the palm lovingly. 'You don't need to see, Josh—touch.'

'Touch . . .?' he repeated shakily.

'Yes,' she buried her face in the dark hair on his chest, kissing his burning flesh.

'God, yes!' he groaned, his hand moving from her face to her breast, feeling each firm contour through her clothing. 'You feel so *good*, Erin,' he moaned.

'So do you,' she told him shyly, slipping the shirt from his broad shoulders.

'Erin . . .!' His mouth took possession of hers once again, his lips warm and moist, probing between her lips to tell her how deeply he desired her.

Erin was on fire, eagerly helping Josh remove her robe, as his hand probed the vee-neckline of her pyjamas, touching the erect tautness of her nipple. An aching pleasure shot through her limbs, making her knees buckle beneath her, and she burrowed against Josh as he lifted her tenderly

141

into his arms and carried her over to the velvet sheet that
lay over the cushions on the floor, where he put her down
among their softness, slowly undoing the buttons to her
pyjama jacket, spreading it wide to reveal the rosky peaks
of her tender young breasts.

'God, I wish I could see you!' he said once again.

'Total recall, Josh,' she reminded him huskily.
'Remember?'

'Oh, I remember,' he gave a bitter laugh. 'How I remember,' he moaned throatily, bending to kiss her breast
with unerring accuracy, teasing the nipple with the
warmth of his mouth, his tongue moving erotically against
the hardened flesh.

Erin held him against her, her head thrown back with
the tense pleasure he was causing, a burning ache beginning deep down in her body, an unfamiliar ache that
made her move restlessly against him.

Josh's knee moved between her legs, pushing them
gently apart as he came to lie between her thighs, their
bodies moving together in an as yet unfulfilled passion.
Their clothes were a hindrance that they were both impatient to remove, and Josh's hand moved beneath her
pyjama trousers to rest possessively on her hips, caressing
the silken flesh with knowing fingers.

When his hand moved to the single fastening Erin helped
him, sliding her hips out of the cumbersome clothing, hearing a rustle of movement as Josh's denims joined the pile of
clothes thrown carelessly across the room.

When his naked body came to her she knew only
pleasure in his male beauty, her initial gasp of pain caught
between his lips as he kissed her with a passion that soon
aroused her to fever-pitch once again.

He stilled for a moment. 'I wish I could just hold this
moment for ever,' he said in a ragged voice.

But soon they knew they didn't want to hold that

moment at all, as their bodies moved together in searing pleasure, the storm outside nothing compared to the storm of their emotions. For Erin Josh's fiercely tender love-making was a revelation, and her body arched against his as nerve-tingling sensations racked her whole body, their pleasure reaching its intense climax in unison, Josh's voice hoarse against her throat as he groaned his heated satisfaction.

Just at that moment the lights came back on.

Erin buried her face against Josh's shoulder, embarrassment delicately colouring her cheeks.

'Their timing's a bit off,' he chuckled softly. 'But it could have been worse.'

It certainly could! The shock of what had just happened between them suddenly hit her. She had been too overwhelmed with the intensity of her love to deny what they both wanted, but now the consequences of her actions washed over her.

For Josh it had just been another enjoyable physical experience, no words of love had passed his lips even at the most intense moment of their lovemaking, whereas it had just deepened the love she felt for him, made her want to cling and cling to him, to never be parted from him again.

The starkness of the electric lighting had brought home to her the seriousness of what had just occurred between them, their bodies still deeply entwined, even though Erin knew they had mentally drawn apart.

'Erin?' Josh looked down at her, smoothing the damp hair from her brow as he supported himself above her with his elbows.

She couldn't meet the enquiry in his eyes. 'I—You're squashing me,' she told him in a husky voice, pushing at the hard wall of his chest.

'I'm sorry.' He instantly moved off her.

Erin sat up to cover her nakedness. 'Could you pass me my clothes please?'

He frowned his puzzlement at her behaviour. 'Erin——'

'Please, Josh!' Her tone was sharp, selfconscious of her nudity.

'Okay,' and he gave a resigned shrug, standing up in one fluid movement to collect her clothes together.

Erin watched him beneath lowered lashes, knowing she had never seen a man as beautiful as Josh, not even those muscular type they insisted on putting in advertisements. Josh moved with a surefooted grace, feeling no embarrassment at his own nakedness—and no wonder, he had a magnificent body, sleek and powerful. And minutes earlier he had given her pleasure with that body, had pleasured her so intensely that she still quivered with the emotion, her limbs seeming to tremble as she pulled on the pyjamas he handed her, tying the belt of her robe with a sense of loss.

Lovemaking shouldn't end like this, even in her inexperience she knew that. They should be in each other's arms, murmuring words of love to each other, anticipating making love once again. Instead of which they were eyeing each other warily, Josh pushing the bottom of his shirt into his denims before buckling his belt.

He put a hand up to his eyes, running it around to his nape. 'What do you want me to say?' He looked at her with darkened eyes.

She wanted him to tell her he loved her! That he couldn't live without her, that she meant everything to him. She wanted him to ask her to *marry* him!

'Nothing,' she said dully. 'I think it would be better if we both said nothing.'

He gave a deep sigh. 'If that's what you want.'

'It is.'

'I'm sorry, Erin.'

That was the one thing she hadn't wanted him to say! It only confirmed her belief that he regretted making love to her, that he probably regretted ever meeting her.

Her mouth trembled precariously as she held back the tears. 'Goodnight, Josh.' She ran to the door, desperate to get to her room before she burst into loud sobs. She had never looked pretty when she cried, had never seen anyone who did, and she could do without that added blow to her self-esteem.

'Erin!' He stopped her at the door. 'Erin, I——'

'Nothing, Josh,' she reminded him. 'Please—nothing.'

'I—I'm just so damned sorry!' He looked ill.

'So am I,' she choked before running to her room, where she leaned heavily back against the door, tears already streaming down her face before she began to sob in earnest.

Waking up the next morning was the hardest thing she ever had to do, not wanting to remember the ecstasy of being loved by Josh the night before—or his regret afterwards.

She was halfway through dressing when Josh knocked on the door and entered the room. Erin froze in the action of buttoning her shirt, hastily doing up the remaining buttons as she realised a vast expanse of bare flesh and the silky smooth material of her bra must be visible to Josh's narrow-eyed gaze.

They continued to look at each other warily, neither of them seeming to know what to say to the other.

'I—I'm sorry I missed our ride this morning,' Erin finally spoke. 'I didn't feel in the mood.' She hadn't felt she could face him, accompany him on the ride as if nothing had happened between them last night. They both knew they could never go back to that innocence.

'I didn't go myself. I wasn't in the mood either,' he

shrugged dismissal of the subject. 'Do you want breakfast?'

'No—thank you.' She doubted she would be able to get anything down her throat. 'Maybe some coffee. But I'll get you something to eat if you want it,' she added, belatedly remembering that was part of the reason she was here.

'I've already eaten.' He eyed her suitcase that stood in the corner of the room. 'Is that packed?'

She gave a startled frown. 'It's never been *un*packed, it didn't seem worth it.'

'Good,' Josh nodded. 'I'm taking you to Martha and Jim's for a few days. If you——'

'You're what!' She stood up, hastily tucking her shirt into the waistband of her denims. 'Josh, if this is because of last night——'

'I thought you didn't want to talk about it,' he ground out.

'I don't——'

'Then we won't.'

'But if that's the reason you're sending me away——'

'I'm not sending you away,' he rasped his impatience. 'I just—I'm going to be—busy for the next couple of days. You might as well spend that time with Martha.'

'But——'

'You've been on your own nearly all week, and it's going to get worse,' he warned. 'I happen to think you would be better off with Martha.'

'But who's going to take care of you?'

His mouth twisted mockingly. 'I managed pretty well on my own before you came. But as it happens,' he added briskly, 'I'm not going to be here.'

'You're going away?' Her face must have revealed her dismay, and she quickly masked the emotion. It was obvious Josh didn't want her around any more. She was an embarrassment to him now, a reminder that he had made love to her in the heat of the moment, desire getting the better of good sense.

'Not exactly. But I'm going to be too busy to worry about anyone taking care of me.'

She would rather he were honest and just told her he found her presence here awkward, that she made him feel uncomfortable. 'Okay, I'll go,' she said dully. 'I'm ready to go now, if you are.' She picked up her jacket and suit-case.

'Give that to me,' Josh took the case out of her hand. 'Erin, this—last night doesn't change anything, I'll still take you to England with me.'

Why not—she had fully earned her ticket now! 'Fine,' she nodded. 'Will Martha be expecting me?'

'I called her——'

'It must have been early.' It was only eight-thirty now! Josh shrugged. 'They're early risers.'

She gave a falsely bright smile. 'We'd better get going, then.'

'Yes.' He seemed about to say something else, then changed his mind and walking out to the truck, the faithful Sheba at his heels.

Erin hunched miserably on her side of the truck, seeing nothing, feeling nothing but the pain of being parted from Josh. She had thought that she at least had the rest of the week with him, but now she wasn't even to have that. And it was at Josh's own instigation.

She must have been glaringly obvious the night before, must have shown her love for him in a thousand different ways. An affair was one thing, but a clinging woman in love was something else completely!

At last she looked up, hoping her voice would be steady. 'What reason did you give Martha and Jim for my staying with them?' Fortunately her voice sounded cool, and only faintly interested.

Josh only glanced at her, his expression grim. 'The truth—I told them the truth.'

She gasped. 'You told them about——'

'I told them I was going to be busy,' he interrupted dryly. 'They understood perfectly.'

As she was supposed to, no doubt. How many other lovesick girls had he pushed on to his friends when they became too clinging?

'I'll enjoy being with Martha,' she told him brightly. 'I've missed female company.'

'I'm sure,' he said tersely. 'Get off, Sheba!' he snapped at the dog as she nuzzled against his arm.

Erin sympathised with the poor dog as she gazed up at her master with adoring eyes. Now the two of them had had their love thrown back in their faces!

'Sheba will be staying with you,' he told her as he stopped the truck outside the ranch-house.

'Oh, but——'

'I won't have the time to look after her,' he said abruptly, as he got out to collect her case from the back.

'Surely you aren't going to be that busy,' she protested, following him.

'I am.' His tone was uncompromising.

'It must be nice to thrust the people who love you out of your life whenever you feel like it,' she said bitterly.

His eyes narrowed. 'Meaning?'

'Meaning Sheba!' she said in an agitated voice. 'She isn't going to understand being left here.' As she didn't! She longed to throw her arms about his throat and beg him to let her stay with him. But she wouldn't do it, couldn't do it.

'She understands better than you think,' he assured her dryly. 'Ah, Martha,' he turned to smile at his cousin. 'It's good of you to take Erin at such short notice.'

'Not at all,' she smiled warmly. 'I'll enjoy the company.

And in the circumstances——'

'Yes,' Josh cut in tersely, warningly it seemed to Erin's sensitive ears. 'Well, I'll have to get back now . . .'

'Of course,' Martha nodded. 'Don't worry about Erin, she'll be fine here with us.'

'I know,' he smiled, and turned to Erin, the smile still in his warm green eyes. 'Take care, sweetheart,' he said huskily. 'And don't worry, I'll be back to pick you up before you know it.'

She doubted that, she was missing him already! And she knew the endearment had been for his cousin's sake, but she couldn't help revelling in it anyway.

'I have to go now, Erin,' he added deeply, cupping either side of her face as he looked down at her with intense green eyes. 'I'll be back as soon as I can.'

'I—I hope so.' She risked embarrassing him one more time. 'I—Sheba will miss you,' she gave a nervous smile, hoping she didn't cry before he left her.

His thumbtips caressed her trembling lower lip. 'I hope she isn't the only one,' he gave a rueful smile. 'You try and miss me too, hmm?'

'I—I'll try.' Her voice shook.

'That's all I ask.' He bent and kissed her lingeringly on the lips, turning to his cousin as he straightened. 'I'll be in touch,' he said abruptly, moving away from Erin.

Martha nodded. 'Take care.'

' 'Bye, girl.' He bent to pet Sheba, the dog's tail wagging once more. 'Take care of your mistress for me,' he murmured.

Erin blinked dazedly, sure that she must have misheard him. Josh must have said, 'Take care of *my* mistress for me'. And she resented it. One night of passion together didn't make her *anyone's* mistress.

'I can take care of myself,' she told him tartly. 'I always have.'

'Yes,' he nodded. 'Tell Jim I'll see him later,' he told his cousin before leaving.

'Come into the house,' Martha invited softly as Erin stared numbly after the departing truck. 'We'll have some coffee. And I'm sure you can't have had any breakfast. Josh must have rushed you over here so fast you barely had time to pack,' she scolded, taking Erin inside.

'I—I——' To her shame Erin burst into tears, her face buried in her hands as she sobbed out her misery.

Martha put her arms comfortingly about her, holding her until the worst of the crying had passed. 'Come and sit down,' she soothed. 'Men!' she added disgustedly once Erin was safely seated in one of the armchairs. 'Miss him, indeed, when anyone can see you're breaking your heart for him!'

'I'm not——'

'Oh yes, you are,' the other girl insisted. 'And fool that he is, he can't even see it.'

'And I don't want him to,' Erin sniffed, wiping the tears from her cheeks. 'Promise you won't tell him?'

'But——'

'Please, Martha. I didn't mean to cry just now, it's just that——'

'You love him.'

'No——'

'Oh yes,' Martha nodded gently. 'Don't worry, Erin, I won't tell Josh. If he's too blind to see it for himself then maybe he doesn't deserve to know.'

'Thanks.' She gave a wan smile. 'Now what did you say about coffee? Josh did rush me out of the house without any this morning.'

'Typical!' his cousin laughed. 'Come into the kitchen and we can talk while I cook you breakfast.'

Despite missing Josh so much she spent an enjoyable day with his cousin. Jim's welcome was friendly too when he came home later that evening, although he looked exhausted, and he was filthy dirty.

'How is it?' his wife asked anxiously.

'Still blazing.' Jim sat down wearily. 'They're doing their best, but unless the wind changes . . . I don't even like to think about it.' He put his hands over his eyes.

'Josh?' Martha asked anxiously.

'Still out there,' he sighed. 'Not that there's anything we can do, but——'

'Out where?' Erin suddenly interrupted, her expression as anxious as Martha's. 'Out where?' she repeated desperately as no one seemed inclined to answer her.

'Oh dear!' Martha bit her top lip. 'I—We—You see, Josh didn't want to worry you.'

'Erin doesn't know?' Jim groaned his dismay.

'No. You see——'

'No, I don't *see* at all, Martha,' Erin said tautly. 'What doesn't Josh want me to worry about? And where is he?' Her voice rose shrilly over the last.

'The electric storm last night,' Jim sighed. 'It caused a lot of forest fires,' he grimaced, 'and one of them is heading this way. Josh's house, and consequently this one too, are directly in its path.'

'Oh no . . .' she paled to a sickly grey. 'And—and Josh is—out there, trying to stop it?' She hardly dared ask the question, already knowing the answer. Josh wasn't the type of man to sit back and take it when he was threatened, in any way. He would go down fighting, even against a forest fire.

'Not stop it exactly,' Jim pulled a face. 'Just trying to help the people who are trying. It looks pretty hopeless, the fire has got too great a hold.'

'But you said something about the wind changing?' She looked from one to the other of them. 'Didn't you?' she demanded anxiously.

'Yes,' Jim nodded. 'It's predicted by the weathermen, and they're digging a fire-break in the hope that it does happen. If the wind hasn't changed direction in the next forty-eight hours they'll start evacuating us from the area.'

'But your homes . . .'

'Will go up in smoke,' Martha said simply.

'But I—I don't understand. How can you just sit there and accept it?' Erin's expression was frantic.

'We aren't just sitting back and accepting it!' Jim stood up impatiently. 'Josh and I have been out there all day trying to stop it, Josh is still trying.'

'I'm sorry.' She was instantly contrite. 'It's just—Is Josh in any danger?'

'No——'

'I want the truth,' she said firmly. 'I'm not a child. Josh had no right to keep it from me.'

Jim sighed. 'The truth is that we just don't know. All forest fires are dangerous.'

'I want to go to him! I want——'

'No,' Jim told her quietly.

'I—No?'

'No,' he repeated. 'Josh's last words to me were that under no circumstances were you to return to the bungalow.'

'I see,' she bit her lip. 'I—If you don't mind I think I'll go to my room.'

'Erin——'

She didn't heed Martha's distressed cry, shutting herself in the bedroom they had given her for her stay. Why couldn't she accept, once and for all, that Josh just didn't want her around, not even during this crisis?

The next two days seemed endless as they waited for word that the wind had changed or that they had to leave the ranch.

On the third day Jim returned at lunch-time dirty and dishevelled as usual, but with a boyish grin to his dirt-covered features. 'It's finished!' he cried, swinging Martha round in his arms excitedly. 'The fire's out!'

'I—But how?' Erin had come through to the kitchen as soon as she heard Jim's unexpected arrival.

'For once the weathermen were right, the wind changed more or less on time. When it hit the dug-out area it just started to go out,' Jim explained. 'It's just about over now.'

'Oh, thank God!' she sighed her relief. 'Josh . . .?'

'He's fine,' the other man reassured her. 'Tired, like me, but otherwise fine.'

'When can I go to the bungalow?' she asked excitedly. 'I realise Josh probably wanted to sleep right now, but he'll be coming for me after dinner, won't he?'

'Er——'

She hid her disappointment, seeing denial in Jim's face. 'Tomorrow morning will do as well. I——'

'Erin,' Jim got her attention, 'Josh isn't coming for you at all.'

'Not coming?' she blinked dazedly. 'Then you're going to take me back—aren't you?' The last came out weakly as Jim shook his head. 'Why aren't you?' she asked dully.

'Josh think's it would be better if you stayed here,' he told her gently. 'He——'

'He doesn't want me with him.' She straightened her shoulders as if warding off a blow. 'Right, I'll stay at a motel in town.'

'You most certainly will not,' Martha said indignantly. 'I won't hear of it!'

'Neither will I,' Jim put in firmly. 'It isn't a question of Josh not wanting you with him, Erin. He's going to be helping them clear some of the mess the fire has caused, he won't even be home half the time. And the other half he'll be sleeping,' he added as she went to protest. 'If you leave here he'll come looking for you,' he warned.

He would too. He would feel responsible for seeing she got back to England. It couldn't be soon enough for her.

By Saturday she had given up hope of seeing Josh before they went to England the next day, and then she found she was to see him after all.

'Josh is coming to dinner tonight,' Martha told her as she prepared the steaks for cooking.

Colour instantly flooded Erin's pale cheeks. 'He is?' She licked her lips nervously.

'Mm. That will be nice, won't it?' Martha gave her an encouraging smile.

Considering she hadn't seen him for a week it would be more than 'nice'! 'I suppose so,' Erin forced herself to sound casual.

Not that Martha and Jim could be in any doubt as to her feelings towards Josh, that had been patently obvious by her preoccupation all week. The young couple had been very friendly, very kind, but she couldn't help missing Josh.

When she heard him arrive just after five she deliberately made herself linger in her bedroom. Martha and Jim might be aware of the fact that she loved Josh, but he certainly wasn't going to know about it too!

She walked into the lounge about ten minutes after she had heard him arrive, looking at him beneath lowered lashes. He looked just the same, so handsome he made her breath catch in her throat, although he looked tired too. The fire had exhausted both men; Erin had witnessed Jim's weariness for herself, and Josh still looked tired, pale beneath the tan of his skin, lines of fatigue about his eyes.

'You're looking well,' he told her huskily, his gaze lingering on her bare midriff, her shirt tied just below her breasts, the same pretty pink as the pink flowers in her black and pink wrap-around skirt, her bare feet thrust into low black sandals.

'Thank you,' she accepted. 'I wish I could return the compliment . . .'

His mouth twitched, and finally he smiled openly. 'As honest as ever, I see.'

'Of course.' She sat down beside him on the sofa, while Martha and Jim suddenly excused themselves to go and cook the food on the barbecue.

'I think they're being tactful,' Josh drawled, his arm resting lightly along the back of the sofa.

'Really?' Erin feigned uninterest. 'I can't imagine why.'

'Can't you?' His voice was husky.

'No.' She gave a casual shrug and stood up. 'I'll go and help Martha. I'm sure you and Jim must have plenty to talk about.'

His eyes narrowed as he looked up at her. 'And we don't?'

'Not that I know of,' she replied coolly. 'Sheba's outside, by the way.'

He nodded. 'I saw her on the way in. She looks well. You did a good job of taking care of her.'

'I didn't——'

'Jim told me she's rarely left your side.'

'She missed you,' Erin shrugged.

'And you, did you miss me?'

'At first I suppose I did.' She made herself smile, determined Josh wouldn't know she had stupidly fallen in love with him. 'But Martha and Jim are such good company that I soon got over it.'

His expression was harsh. 'You'll be glad to leave tomorrow, then,' he ground out.

She swallowed hard. 'It will be nice to see England again,' she evaded, knowing that tomorrow would be the end as far as they were concerned.

'Then we'll have to make sure you take home one last good memory of Canada,' Josh said grimly. 'As Dave told you, the Calgary Stampede isn't to be missed.'

Erin licked her lips nervously. 'We're going to the Stampede?'

'Tonight,' he nodded.

'I—I didn't know.'

He shrugged. 'I wasn't sure I could make it, so I told Martha and Jim not to mention it to you.'

'Like you told them not to tell me about the fire,' she recalled bitterly.

'I had no idea what your reaction would be——'

'I'm not the hysterical type,' she snapped. She drew in a deep, steadying breath. When Martha had told her Josh was coming here tonight she had decided that she wouldn't become emotional. She wasn't making a very good job of keeping to that decision! 'Still, the Stampede will be nice,' she added lightly.

'I hope so,' he said tersely.

If she sparkled throughout the meal, talking and laughing happily, then Josh just became grimmer by the minute, scowling at them all by the time they had finished eating.

'I'm looking forward to the Stampede,' she told him eagerly as they drove into Calgary later that evening, Martha and Jim apparently having tickets to go later in the week.

'So I gathered,' Josh said dryly, very casually dressed in denims and a checked shirt, his hat pushed to the back of his black hair.

Erin still wore her blouse and skirt, the evening very warm. 'Sorry,' she muttered, falling into a moody silence.

It was a silence that neither of them seemed anxious to break, although Erin couldn't help but be affected by everyone's mood of enjoyment once they entered the Stampede Grounds where the Stampede was being held—

people of all ages enjoying the infectious gaiety of the huge funfair, the sideshows, the numerous exhibitions of live-stock, the chuckwagon racing about to take place in the Stadium itself.

Josh took hold of her hand as they walked through the crowds of people, his height and breadth instantly making them a pathway. 'We're going to watch the chuckwagon racing first,' he told her abruptly. 'Then we'll go round the fair and sideshows.'

She felt sure the latter was for her, and she resented his condescension. 'I'm not a child,' she snapped.

'Maybe not, but I am, about funfairs,' Josh grinned down at her. 'Truce for tonight, Erin?'

Her love for this man warred with her indignation of being left with his friends all week. Her love won. 'Truce,' she smiled up at him tremulously.

'Good girl!' He kissed her lightly on the nose.

It might be the sort of affectionate gesture a brother would give a sister but nevertheless Erin hugged that kiss to her, laughing happily when Josh bought her one of the straw stetsons on sale at the kiosks at the fair.

'Now you look like a native Calgarian,' he smiled as he placed the hat on her blonde hair. 'It suits you.'

'Then why are you laughing?'

'Because you look cute.'

Warm pleasure shot through her body, although she still had the feeling of a child being humoured.

The chuckwagon racing was exciting, as Dave had said it was, although Erin cringed a little as one of the wagons overturned, clutching anxiously at Josh's arm.

'It's okay,' his eyes were narrowed against the glare of the sun, 'Lance will be all right, he knows how to get out of these tight situations. There,' he pointed as the driver of the wagon rolled from underneath it, running to the side of the arena to avoid the pounding hooves as the four horses pulling the driverless wagon thundered out on to the circular racetrack into the path of the other three wagons in this heat. 'He's fine, probably a bit bruised, but otherwise all right.'

'But the wagon——'

'Will be stopped by the officials,' Josh assured her.

It was too. Lighter than the other wagons because of its lack of a driver, the blue-coloured wagon easily took the lead, headed off by two officials on horseback before it could hinder the other wagons, and pulled off to one side as the race continued.

'You seem to know a lot about it,' Erin said curiously.

He shrugged. 'I used to be one of the outriders.'

Her eyes widened. The chuckwagon had to be loaded up with a stove and a tent before doing a figure eight around barrels, the stove and tent put into the wagon by the three outriders at the back, a fourth man holding the horses steady at the front of the wagon while trying to hold the reins of his own horse too. Once the wagon had been loaded the four outriders could get on their horses and follow behind the speeding wagon. And they didn't always make it! She had seen a couple of them tumble to the ground, one of them seeming quite badly hurt as he clutched his trampled ribs.

'Were you ever hurt?' she asked worriedly.

'Only once. I broke my arm.'

She swallowed hard. 'How?'

'I went under the horse,' Josh shrugged. 'The next heat is about to start.' He pointed as the four new wagons came out on to the track, ready to start the fifth of the eight heats.

'I—I think I've seen enough,' said Erin through stiff lips. 'Could we go now?'

Josh turned to her concernedly. 'You're very pale, aren't you feeling well?'

'I—No, I don't think I am.' The thought of him going under the pounding of a horse's hoofs made her feel ill. He could have been killed!

'Then of course we'll leave.' He took hold of her elbow and guided her out of the stadium. 'Maybe a drink would make you feel better?' he suggested once they were back outside.

'Maybe,' Erin nodded. 'Perhaps a Coke or something?'

'Sure.' He went to one of the kiosks, coming back with two huge paper cups.

Erin sipped uninterestedly at the Coke. 'Why did you become an outrider?' she asked suddenly.

Josh frowned. 'Why did I——?' He shrugged. 'Jim's father used to be one of the drivers, Jim and I would be two of his outriders.'

'But why?' she persisted.

'Why not? It was fun, very exciting—and I got paid for it,' he added with a smile. 'I wasn't always the affluent artist you see today,' he taunted. 'When I was a student I never had any money. Whenever we could Jim and I would ride for his father, and anyone else who could use us. Sometimes I earned fifty dollars a night. You can earn almost three times that much now.'

'But it's dangerous!'

'Most of life is,' he shrugged.

'And Jim's father, was he ever hurt?'

Josh grimaced. 'I was hoping you wouldn't ask me that. About five years ago he crashed badly, breaking his pelvis and both his legs.'

'He's in a wheelchair . . .' she shuddered.

'Nothing as serious as that. He does have a limp, though. And it was because of his injuries that Jim's mother pleaded with him to give it up. Hey,' he chided, 'are we here to enjoy ourselves or not? I thought you wanted to go round the sideshows.'

'I do,' she decided firmly. 'Yes, I do.' She threw her empty cup into a bin.

'Feeling better now?' Josh put a companionable arm about her shoulders.

'Much.' She gave a bright smile. 'What are you going to win me first?' She looked at the game sideshows, all of them displaying huge cuddly toys. But as she knew from experience, it was virtually impossible to win any of them.

Josh grinned at her, looking relaxed and almost boyish. 'If that's a challenge, I accept.'

'Go ahead,' she smiled back.

Much to her surprise he won her several of the smaller cuddly toys, the three and four-foot ones seeming out of reach, their fluffy gay colours inviting as they hung suspended from the kiosk roofs.

'Never mind,' Erin said happily, holding on to the four ridiculous toys Josh had already won her. 'I don't think I could carry any more anyway.'

'But you wanted one, and I'm going to get you one if it takes all night,' he said firmly.

'No, Josh——'

'Yes.'

It didn't take him all night, it took him about ten minutes to have the assistant untie one of the three-and-a-half-foot bears from the roof, handing it to Erin as she handed the smaller toys to Josh to carry, beaming her gratitude at him. No one had ever won her anything in her life, and she held on to it like a child with a cherished toy.

'Did you enjoy your first Stampede?' They walked slowly back to the side street where they had parked the truck.

'I loved it,' she glowed.

'I'm glad. Although he looks more like an elephant than a bear with those huge ears.' Josh teasingly eyed the cuddly toy it was taking Erin all her time to carry.

'He doesn't have a trunk,' she defended indignantly.

'Bears don't have ears like that,' Josh derided.

She gave him an outraged look. 'I think he's lovely!'

He grinned. 'I wonder what they'll make of him at the airport tomorrow.'

Her happiness suddenly evaporated. Tomorrow—tomorrow they flew to England.

CHAPTER NINE

Martha and Jim were still up when they got back to the ranch. 'Goodness!' Martha laughed as she saw Erin laden down with the toys. 'I don't need to ask if you had a good time!'

'It was lovely,' Erin confirmed.

'Here,' Josh held out some caramel popcorn to Martha, 'I know you have a passion for it,' he grinned.

'Oh, thank you!' She hugged him.

'Are you trying to make my wife fat?' Jim laughed as Martha gave him an indignant look. 'Don't worry, sweetheart, you'll never be fat.'

'Would anyone mind if I went to bed?' Erin asked them. 'I'm feeling rather tired.' It had been an emotional evening, and now she just wanted to be alone.

'I have to be going now,' Josh answered her. 'Come outside and see me off?' he raised a questioning eyebrow.

'I—Yes.' She glanced at the expectant Martha and Jim. 'Of course.' Josh was obviously still keeping up a pretence in front of his friends, although after the way he had ignored her existence this last week it seemed a rather pointless exercise to her.

'Did you really enjoy yourself tonight?' he asked as they stood next to the pick-up.

She nodded. 'It was fun.'

'I'm glad.' His hands lightly grasped her shoulders. 'Good night, Erin. I'll pick you up around ten in the morning.' He kissed her lightly on the mouth. 'Your last night in Canada. Not been a very happy stay for you, has it?' he said ruefully, his forehead resting lightly on hers.

How could she tell him she never wanted to leave, that she just wanted to stay here with him for the rest of her life? 'Not very,' she agreed huskily. 'But you've been—kind.'

'Kind, hell!' he dismissed grimly. 'You know damned well that I haven't been kind at all, that I——'

'I still don't want to talk about the other night, Josh.' She moved coolly away from him.

'No, I don't suppose you do,' he sighed. 'I don't think I do either. I'll see you in the morning.'

'Yes.' She turned and walked back into the house before he had even got into his truck.

'Everything okay?' Martha looked up from eating her popcorn.

'Fine,' Erin gave a jerky smile. 'I—Goodnight,' and she rushed from the room, wondering if there would ever come a time when the pain would stop.

She was already in bed pretending to be asleep when Martha knocked softly on the door and came in. 'Oh,' she hesitated, 'I didn't realise. You seemed—upset?'

Erin peered at her over the covers. 'Just tired.'

'Are you sure?'

'Sure,' she nodded, not daring to say much in case her voice gave away her tears.

'You and Josh haven't—argued?'

'No,' she answered truthfully.

'I don't mean tonight, Erin,' Martha came to sit on the side of the bed. 'I meant before. It isn't like Josh to ignore a guest, and——'

'I'm not exactly a guest,' Erin said dryly.

The other girl's cheeks coloured delicately. 'I realised that. It's just that——'

'I would really rather not talk about it.' Oh dear, she was beginning to sound like a record stuck in a groove!

'All right,' Martha stood up. 'But—well, I'm sure that

whatever it was Josh wished it had never happened.'

How right she was! Erin almost choked with the irony of it. Martha had hoped to make her feel better, and all she had done was make her feel worse! 'I'm sure he does too,' she agreed huskily. 'Don't worry, Martha, we'll work it out.'

'I hope so,' Martha frowned. 'I hate to see you both so miserable.'

Erin lay awake long into the night, dreading the flight tomorrow, and not through any fear of flying.

Josh's appearance the next day came as something of a surprise to her. He was dressed in a suit! And he looked completely different, more sophisticated, more the famous artist that he was.

The suit was a dark grey pinstripe, three-piece, his shirt snowy white, a light grey tie tied meticulously at his throat. He no longer looked like Josh but was now every inch Joshua Hawke, celebrity.

He wasn't driving the pick-up today either, but driving the Porsche, as far as Erin knew, for the first time since she had been here. He put her case on the back seat with his own, although the huge bear took up most of the room.

He smiled. 'You're really taking that with you?'

'Of course,' she said indignantly, glad she was wearing one of her prettiest summer dresses. She wouldn't have wanted to shame him by wearing her denims.

'And this?' He held up the straw stetson he had given her the evening before.

'Yes.' She was taking everything he had ever given her, including the most wonderful experience of a lifetime, although that would have to stay locked away in her memory, only taken out when she was alone, each comment, each caress, a cherished memory.

Josh shrugged, loading the car up. 'We'd better be on

our way, our plane leaves in just under two hours.'

It was hard to say goodbye to Martha and Jim, knowing she would never see them again, although Martha extracted a promise from her to write to them. She knew she would keep that promise, if only in the hope that Martha would occasionally mention Josh in her own letters.

Being a passenger on a plane accompanied by Joshua Hawke was certainly an experience. From the moment they checked in at the desk Erin found out what it was like to be one of the famous.

They were shown into the first class lounge—Erin learned for the first time that they were travelling first class!—plied with drinks until it was time to board the plane, and the stewardess's smile was particularly warm as she personally escorted them to their seats.

'If you need anything, just ask,' the girl told Josh softly.

'I'll bet,' Erin muttered as the other girl moved away.

Josh turned to look at her. 'Did you say something?'

'Not a thing,' she snapped.

'I thought you did.'

'Well, I didn't! Would you mind if I had a nap now, I'm feeling tired.'

Josh frowned. 'But you've only just got up.'

'And now I'm feeling tired!' Her eyes flashed, her jealousy of the other girl was getting the better of her.

'Have you been eating? Martha said you have, but——'

'Did you check up on me?' she gasped.

'I merely asked——'

'You did!' she glared her fury. 'When will you believe that I don't have that damned illness! I'm not your sister, Josh. I'm me, Erin Richards, and I don't need you watching over me every minute of the day!'

His eyes were cold. 'Obviously not.'

'Definitely not!'

'Then that's settled.'

'Yes!'

They were glaring as if they hated each other. What would have happened next Erin had no idea, but the stewardess came over to offer them both champagne.

Champagne at eleven-thirty in the morning! She refused, and turned away, closing her eyes as if in sleep.

But she wasn't asleep. Every flirtatious remark the stewardess made was audible to her, as were Josh's replies, his voice deep and attractive as he flirted back.

The two of them barely spoke through the whole flight. Inside Erin was crying, on the outside she was acting like a shrew. No wonder Josh preferred to spend most of his time talking to the pretty stewardess!

Leaving the Customs as Heathrow Airport was another revelation to her, although after the preferential treatment Josh had received on the plane the presence of the press at the airport shouldn't really have been such a surprise to her.

Lights flashed, cameras clicked as Josh was bombarded with questions. And all the time he maintained a firm hold on her elbow, refusing to let her leave his side.

'Could we have the name of your companion, Mr Hawke?'

'Did the two of you meet on the plane or did you fly over together?'

'Is this your fiancée, Mr Hawke?'

'Or possibly your wife?' asked another hopeful reporter.

'Mr Hawke——'

Josh looked at them with steely green eyes, his manner composed, despite the jostling going on around them. 'Confine your questions to my professional life and you might get some answers,' he advised curtly.

'Oh, but——'

'Surely you wouldn't mind——'

'She's a lovely young lady, Mr Hawke, and——'

'Yes, she is,' the last man was given a narrow-eyed look, 'and your personal questions will not be answered by either of us.' He walked through their midst, Erin still held firmly at his side. 'Damn then to hell!' he swore under his breath.

Erin almost had to run to keep up with him, as the reporters were left far behind. 'I'm sorry if I've caused you any embarrassment.'

'*You* haven't,' he snapped abruptly, his expression grim. 'Let's get out of here.' He looked for an exit.

'Mr Hawke——'

He turned with a savagery that Erin could feel in the tension of his hand. 'I thought I told you——'

'I'm Gerald Parker, Mr Hawke—Mr Smythe sent me,' the little man explained hastily, eyeing Josh apprehensively.

'Sorry,' Josh sighed. 'Come on, Erin.'

She followed as if in a daze, to be helped into the back of the waiting limousine by a suddenly preoccupied Josh, the other man getting in beside him while the chauffeur loaded their luggage into the boot of the car, Erin's huge bear included. She almost giggled with the haughty disdain with which the chauffeur viewed the latter.

Josh and the man who had introduced himself as Gerald Parker seemed to have a lot to talk about. From their conversation Erin gathered Gerald Parker was an employee of the gallery where Josh's exhibition was to take place, Matthew Smythe, the owner of the gallery.

'He was so sorry he couldn't be here to meet you himself,' Gerald Parker told Josh. 'Unfortunately Mrs Smythe chose this morning to give birth to their first child. So annoying,' he tutted.

Erin watched Josh trying to hide a smile as he made a suitable reply; Gerald Parker's taste obviously did not run in a female direction, and the arrival of a baby was a great inconvenience to him.

'I've booked both of you into a hotel as you asked, Mr Hawke,' he twittered. He was a man of middle age, with sparse brown hair and a meticulous way of dressing, his dark suit and white shirt impeccable. It made Erin wonder what he would have made of the way Josh dressed in Canada. 'A suite,' he added pointedly, giving Erin a curious glance.

'Thanks,' Josh accepted curtly. 'I don't believe I introduced you to Miss Richards.'

'No,' Gerald Parker leant forward to shake her hand. 'Any friend of Mr Hawke's . . .'

'And that's all she is, Parker,' Josh put in coldly. 'I would appreciate your keeping her name out of your scandal sheets.'

'Scandal sheets . . .?'

'The English newspapers,' he explained tersely, taking hold of Erin's hand. 'Miss Richards' name is not to be released to the press.'

'Oh, but——'

'Do I make myself clear?'

'I—Yes. But——'

'Good.' Josh stretched his long legs out in front of him. 'I know Matt and his damned publicity,' he scowled.

'Oh, but I'm sure he wouldn't——'

Josh gave a taunting laugh. 'And I'm equally sure that he would. Any press release about myself and Miss Richards and I'll remove my paintings from the gallery.'

Erin gasped. 'Josh——'

'Understand, Parker?' He gave the other man a cold look.

'Certainly, Mr Hawke.' Gerald Parker was becoming flustered. 'I'll see to it.'

'You do that,' Josh drawled. 'Now, how are the mother and baby?'

'Mother and——? Oh, you mean Mrs Smythe. I think she's well.'

'And the baby?'

'A boy, I think.'

Josh's mouth twitched. 'You don't sound very sure.'

'Well, I—I—They all look the same at that age, don't they?' Gerald Parker twittered.

'Do they?'

'Well, I——'

'Of course they do,' Erin cut in to support Gerald Parker, knowing Josh was enjoying tormenting him and feeling a bit sorry for him. 'Josh, about the hotel——'

His hand tightened painfully about hers. 'We'll talk about it later, Erin.'

'But——'

'Later,' he repeated firmly.

This was a different Josh from the one she was used to, still as autocratic, but now possessing a haughty command that had men like Gerald Parker quaking in their shoes. It was like being presented with another Josh, one it would take a lifetime to know. And she only had a few hours left!

Gerald Parker left them at the hotel, where the receptionist and porter almost fell over themselves when they learned Josh's name—and a hotel like this was used to dealing with celebrities every day!

The suite was everything Erin had ever imagined it would be, although Josh seemed to accept their surroundings without a second glance.

He was on the telephone now, having flowers sent to Ginny Smythe; the name of the hospital she was at, at least, was known to Gerald Parker. He put the telephone down, turning. 'I suppose you'd like to rest,' he said huskily. 'Which bedroom would you like?'

There were four, all of them luxurious in the extreme. 'I can't stay here, Josh. I tried to tell you that in the car——'

'Which room, Erin?' He threw open one of the bedroom doors. 'This one looks okay——'

'I'm not staying,' she said stubbornly, clutching the cuddly bear to her.

'Of course you are.' He scowled. 'And for God's sake put that ridiculous thing down! You look about ten years old.'

'Don't order me about, Josh,' she snapped. 'It may work with Mr Parker, but it won't work with me.'

'Sorry,' he muttered, running a hand through his dark hair. 'When you're put in a jungle you automatically become as aggressive as the other animals.' He sat down wearily. 'Now you know why I only appear in public for three months of the year. It takes me the other nine months to humanise myself again. When I first became famous— and I don't mean that conceitedly—when my paintings were first appreciated, I was just an innocent from Canada. What did I know about exhibitions, promoters, contracts? People walked all over me, took advantage of my ignorance. Attack before you're attacked, Erin, that's the hard lesson I learnt.'

She chewed on her bottom lip, seeing the sense of what he said. 'I'm sorry about that, but I really can't stay here. It wasn't part of our deal.'

He seemed to pale. 'Forget the damned deal!' he rasped. 'I want you to stay here because I care about what happens to you. Did you really think I'd just bring you back to London and dump you?'

'Well, that was the idea——'

'Not mine! You stay with me until I know you have somewhere decent to live and a job to support yourself.'

'But that could take days, weeks!'

'Exactly. How did you think you were going to live, Erin?'

'I—Well, I—I——'

'You stay here,' he told her firmly, standing up. 'Now I want you to get some rest. I have to go to the gallery for a while, but we'll have dinner together when I get back.'

'But——'

'Please, Erin, let me do this for you. God knows I owe you something!'

He was doing this because he felt guilty about making love to her! 'Okay,' she agreed quietly. 'I'll go and rest,' and she turned towards the bedroom.

'Erin . . .!' Josh's hands came down on her shoulders, turning her to face him. 'Erin!' he groaned, and his mouth descended to claim hers, parting her lips gently, the kiss given with slow drugging passion, his face white when he finally released her. 'I'm sorry,' he said jerkily, 'I didn't mean to do that.'

'Then why did you?' she said bitterly.

'Because—because—I'll see you later.' He turned on his heel and left.

As soon as he had gone Erin collected up her belongings and quietly left the hotel, left Josh, not knowing where she was going—and not particularly caring.

CHAPTER TEN

IT was odd to see a picture of yourself in a newspaper, a really strange sensation. It didn't really look like her; the girl in the photograph looked coolly composed, her escort tall and handsome, his hand on her arm wholly possessive.

'Joshua Hawke and his new friend Miss Erin Richards arriving in London yesterday for his latest exhibition', the caption beneath the picture read. There was also a short paragraph beneath this. 'Mr Hawke refused to discuss his relationship with the beautiful Miss Richards, and Miss Richards didn't say anything at all, only gazed up adoringly at the artist. But the couple were reputed to be secluded in a suite at one of London's most famous hotels last night.'

Erin's cheeks had blazed with colour after reading this. Had her adoration of Josh really been so obvious, or was the reporter just embellishing on the truth to make it more of a story? She hoped it was the latter.

After leaving the hotel she booked into a much cheaper one, and the next day she got herself a job in a restaurant in town. The tourist season was still under way, and temporary staff were much in demand.

Luckily no one seemed to connect her with the photograph in the newspapers, probably because they weren't expecting Joshua Hawke's 'friend' to be waiting at table in a restaurant. And that was the way she liked it, wanting to just sink back into obscurity, forget she had ever known someone called Joshua Hawke.

But that wasn't so easy. As the date for his exhibition came closer so more and more appeared about him in the newspapers. Once there had been a photograph of him at a party with a pretty dark-haired woman, and that night Erin cried herself to sleep.

'You don't look well, love,' one of the other waitresses sympathised the next day. 'Maybe you're working too hard. You don't have to do all the overtime Simpkins asks you to, you know.'

She had been working as often as the manager asked her to because when she was at work she couldn't think about Josh. His exhibition was in two days' time, and after that he was supposed to be travelling to Europe, leaving England probably until next year. Erin knew she would have to go to the exhibition, and intended asking for that time off; she knew she had to see the paintings even if she couldn't see the man himself.

She almost dropped the tray of afternoon tea she was carrying when Josh walked into the restaurant. There could be no doubting his knowing she was here, for he walked straight towards her, his expression grim.

It was over a week since she had last seen him, and she gazed hungrily at him, at his animal grace, his handsome face, his air of command.

'What the hell do you mean by walking out on me?' he snapped, his green eyes blazing.

'I——'

He looked about them restlessly. 'Put that damned tray down and let's get out of here. I want to talk to you.'

Her mouth twisted. 'As arrogant as ever, I see.'

'Erin!' he warned in a controlled voice.

She flushed. 'Wait a minute, then.' She delivered the tray, leaving the bill on the table before returning to Josh's side. 'I don't finish for another hour——'

He took hold of her elbow. 'You're finished now,' he told her grimly.

'No——'

'Yes! Go and get your coat, I'll talk to your boss.'

'Josh——'

'Do it, Erin. Or else I'll just drag you out of here.'

One look at his determined expression told that he would too. 'I don't have a coat,' she scorned; the weather was hot. 'And I'll talk to Mr Simpkins myself.' He shouldn't mind her leaving an hour early, not with all the overtime she had been doing for him.

Josh nodded. 'I'll be waiting outside.'

She joined him about five minutes later, her hair now loosened from the clasp at her nape, her light make-up reapplied. Josh didn't even seem to notice her changed appearance, but took her arm and led her over to the limousine that had collected them from the airport, the glass window between them and the driver firmly closed.

'How did you find me?' she turned to ask Josh's grim profile.

'Not easily,' he growled.

She licked her lips nervously. 'But how?'

'Matt had someone look for you.'

Her eyes widened. 'A private detective?' she gasped.

His mouth twisted. 'Nothing so dramatic. Just a friend of his who had the ability to find out where a young girl could disappear to in this town.'

'But why did you want to find me? I mean——'

'You walked out on me!' his eyes were dark. 'I've been worried out of my mind about you. What the hell did you think you were doing, leaving like that?'

She shrugged. 'I thought I was saving you embarrassment——'

'Embarrassment!' he thundered.

'Yes,' Erin sighed. 'I thought the press would leave you alone if I wasn't staying with you. You seemed angry that they might put something about us in the newspapers——'

'I was angry for you, not me.'

'For—for me?'

'Yes. But the damned article appeared anyway,' he scowled.

'Gerald Parker——'

'No, not him, or Matt either. No one at the gallery, otherwise they wouldn't still have my paintings. Someone at the hotel made money out of that little story,' he said grimly.

'You didn't——'

'No, I didn't have them sacked,' he taunted. 'The hotel management—dealt with him themselves.'

'In other words, he was dismissed,' Erin said dryly.

He shrugged. 'I have no idea, but in their shoes that's the action I would take. A place like that can't employ people they can't trust.'

'I suppose not,' she agreed grudgingly. 'Where are we going?' She looked about them curiously.

'To my hotel.'

'No!'

'Oh yes,' Josh told her firmly. 'I want to talk to you, and I don't intend doing it in the back of a car.'

Erin fell silent, letting Josh take hold of her arm as they entered the hotel and went up in the lift to his suite. She owed it to him to at least talk to him; after that she would never see him again.

'Now tell me,' he swung her round to face him as soon as they entered the suite, 'why did you walk out on me?'

'I didn't walk out on you!'

'I don't know what else you'd call it!' he exploded, looking furiously angry. 'Unless of course you *ran*!'

Today he looked more like the Josh from Canada. The formal suit he had worn on the flight over here had been discarded in favour of lightweight black slacks and a dark green shirt, the latter casually unbuttoned down his chest.

Erin still found it difficult to believe that she and this man had made love, that Josh had possessed her, that for long timeless minutes they had been one person.

There was no evidence that Josh even remembered such a time as he continued to glare at her, his eyes deepening in colour at her continued silence.

'Okay, so you couldn't stand being around me any more,' he began to pace the room, 'but you didn't have to leave without telling me, sneak off while I was out.'

'I left you a note.'

'Oh yes,' he scorned. ' "Goodbye, Josh. Thank you",' he quoted. 'Very enlightening!'

Erin shrugged. 'I didn't have anything else to say.'

'No,' he sighed, 'I don't suppose you did. But why didn't you call me, at least let me know you were all right?'

'Because——'

'Because you aren't! You——'

'Will you let me talk!' Her eyes flashed. 'I'm nineteen years old, Josh, and in this country that means I'm an adult.'

'You don't act like one,' he muttered gloweringly.

'Don't I?' Her voice was brittle. 'Don't you consider it adult to walk away from a situation that can only be embarrassing—to both people concerned?'

He seemed to be fighting a battle within himself, seeming about to speak several times and then changing his mind. 'You still could have called me,' he finally mumbled. 'I didn't enjoy having a third party involved in my search for you. But I had no idea how to start looking for you myself.'

'How did he find me?'

'By a lot of hard work,' Josh revealed harshly. 'You could have been dead for all I knew!' His hand shook as he ran it through the dark thickness of his hair.

'Josh——'

'I tried all the hospitals and morgues first,' he told

her in a haunted voice.

'Oh, Josh, you had no need——'

'I had every need, damn you!' he turned on her viciously. 'You were my responsibility——'

'But I didn't want to be—I *don't* want to be. I have somewhere to live, I have a job, and I'm well. There, are you satisfied?' she asked bitterly.

'Are you eating?'

'Oh, for God's sake!' She walked wearily to the door. 'How many times do I have to tell you I am not Sharon? I'm eating, I'm sleeping, I'm surviving without the great Joshua Hawke watching over me. Now can I go?'

'Erin . . .'

'Can I go?' she repeated firmly.

'I suppose so,' he sighed defeatedly.

She turned at the door, hesitating. 'Good luck with your exhibition.'

He gave her a sharp look. 'Aren't you coming?'

She shrugged. 'I may go one day, if I get time.'

'Tomorrow night,' he said abruptly. 'I have a private showing for the critics, buyers, and a few friends. I want you to be there.'

'No——'

'Yes!' he rasped. 'Surely it isn't too much to ask?'

She avoided his searching gaze, not wanting him to know exactly how 'too much' it was. 'I may have to work . . .'

'Please, Erin,' his tone was huskily persuasive. 'I need—I want you to be there.'

She bit her bottom lip, fighting a war within herself, tempted beyond endurance to agree to being able to see him once more, but knowing the pain of parting would only be all the harder to bear. Temptation won. 'All right, I'll come,' she told him softly. 'But after that will you accept that I'm perfectly capable of taking care of myself, that I don't want to be anyone's responsibility?'

'Yes,' he agreed stiffly. 'I'll call for you——'

'No,' she shook her head stubbornly.

'Then I'll send a car for you.'

'I'll make my own way there,' she insisted.

'Erin——'

'Josh!' She met his gaze steadily.

An unwilling grin lightened his features. 'I guess you are an adult after all.'

'I would have thought you already knew that!' The remark came out before she could stop herself, and she bit her lips as his humour faded.

'Yes,' he acknowledged bitterly. 'Seven-thirty tomorrow. You know where the gallery is?'

'I know,' she nodded.

Luckily the next day was pay-day, and Erin used her lunch-hour to go out and buy a new dress, knowing that the people at this party tonight would be important to Josh. And if any of them read the newspapers they would know she had arrived from Canada with him, and she had no intention of embarrassing Josh by arriving looking anything but her best.

She bought a black gown, figure-hugging, with a deep vee between her breasts, their firm swell just visible to anyone who cared to look closely enough. Her hair was newly washed, her make-up light on her tanned skin. She looked young and alluring, and she knew Josh would have no reason to feel ashamed of her appearance.

The gallery was firmly closed to the public until tomorrow, although the man on the door soon showed her inside once she had given him her name. The room was full of people, all of them drinking champagne as they walked from painting to painting. They were as brilliant as always, and she could hear the murmur of appreciation from the other people present.

'Where the hell have you been?'

Erin slowly turned to face Josh, a little surprised by his attitude. 'I've been right here,' she answered calmly, her breath catching in her throat at how attractive he looked in the black evening suit, its cut across his broad shoulders superb.

'For how long?' he scowled.

'About five minutes,' she answered in a puzzled voice.

'You were late,' he accused.

'Only about ten minutes——'

'I should have been told you'd arrived,' he muttered almost to himself.

'Don't be silly, Josh,' she dismissed lightly. 'In this crowd I'm surprised you noticed me at all.'

His eyes suddenly became a deep, dark green. 'Oh, I noticed you. You look beautiful, Erin.'

'Thank you,' she blushed her pleasure.

'I——'

'Josh, Atkins would like to congratulate you.' A man of about thirty appeared at his side.

Josh glowered at him. 'Atkins will have to wait——'

'You mean Adam Atkins?' Erin couldn't resist her gasp of astonishment.

The newcomer looked at her for the first time, his appraisal appreciative. 'I don't think we've been introduced . . .' he said charmingly.

'Erin Richards, Matthew Smythe,' Josh introduced tersely.

Matthew Smythe smiled. 'Of course, I should have recognised you,' he shook his head, his grasp firm.

'Recognised me?' she blinked. 'Oh, of course—the newspapers. I'm not surprised you didn't, I hardly recognised myself,' she returned his smile. 'How are your wife and son?'

'It was a daughter,' Matthew laughed. 'Gerald has

no sense of the occasion.'

' "All babies look alike",' Erin quoted with a laugh, then the laughter died in her throat as Josh scowled down at them. '*Was* it Adam Atkins you were talking about?' she repeated.

'Yes,' Matt nodded. 'He thinks this is Josh's best yet. And I have to agree with him. It's a damned masterpiece.'

'But, Josh, you can't keep a man like that waiting,' Erin told him in a scandalised voice. Adam Atkins was the most renowned critic in the world. He could make or break someone like Josh, despite Josh's own importance. 'You have no need to stay with me,' she assured him. 'I'm just going to have a walk around.'

'Matt——'

'I'll take care of Erin,' the other man offered instantly. 'Atkins is over by——'

'I can see him,' Josh said abruptly. 'Erin, I'll be back in a few minutes. You won't disappear, will you?'

'Of course not.'

'Good.' He bent and kissed her slightly on the mouth before walking over to the art critic, and the two of them instantly became engaged in conversation.

Erin's cheeks were coloured a delicate pink. Why on earth had Josh kissed her in front of all these people? She could see people giving her curious looks even now, and the conversation in the room suddenly seemed all the more intense. And she recognised some of the people present as the reporters who had met them at the airport!

'Josh shouldn't have asked you to stay with me, Mr Smythe,' she said awkwardly. 'I'm sure you must have plenty of other people to talk to. Please feel free to leave me.'

'Certainly not!' He drew her hand through the crook of his arm. 'Let's go and get some champagne and then I'll take you round and introduce you to everyone.'

She accepted the glass of champagne, sipping at the bubbly liquid. 'I'd rather look at Josh's paintings next, if you don't mind,' she said shyly.

He gave her a surprised look. 'You haven't already seen them?'

She gave a light laugh. 'Only on the back of Josh's pick-up, in a crate.'

'Oh, I see,' he nodded. 'In that case I'd be honoured to take you round.'

The paintings were beautiful—about thirty in all, each one a true work of art, most of them depicting the beauty of Canada, one or two of them of the Indians of old, a couple more of a rodeo in action, the bucking horse almost seeming to leap off the canvas.

'And now for the masterpiece everyone is talking about,' Matt said excitedly. 'But of course you've seen that.'

'No, I——' Her denial froze in her throat, all colour draining from her face as she looked at the painting that had place of honour in the gallery, the lights picking up every brush-stroke.

It was the painting of a woman, her skin very white against the blue velvet sheet she reclined on, the sunlight revealing every naked curve, the breasts firm and uptilting, the waist slender, the thighs curving out gently, the legs long and shapely. Only the face was in shadow, turned away from the artist, the features merely hinted at, framed by blonde wavy hair, looking almost gold in the sunlight. Yes, the features were in shadow, but Erin knew the painting to be of herself—and she knew everyone else in the room knew it too! At least it had a 'NOT FOR SALE' notice on it!

She turned blindly, her only thoughts ones of escape. Josh had completed the painting after all, had painted her naked-ness for all to see. And he hadn't called it *Innocence* either; the title beneath the painting had been *Elusive Lover*.

'Erin!' Matthew Smythe grasped her arm. 'Erin, are you all right?'

'Yes,' she told him through stiff lips. 'I—I have to go.'

'Come with me.' He led her into an office, sitting her down in an armchair, taking the glass of champagne out of her numbed fingers. 'I think you need something stronger than that.' He moved to an array of drinks on the sidecupboard. 'Here,' he handed her a glass of brandy.

Erin sipped it, not even noticing the fiery liquid passing down her throat. Josh had painted her naked! Had invited her here to witness her humiliation.

Matt moved to sit on the edge of the desk, watching her concernedly. 'You didn't know, did you?'

'No,' she gave a bitter, choked laugh, 'no, I didn't know.'

'It's a masterpiece, Erin——'

'It's *me*!' she corrected shrilly. 'Me, lying there naked, for all to see!'

'It's you painted through the eyes of someone who loves you——'

'No,' she shook her head, 'it's me painted by someone who lusted after me. *Elusive Lover*,' she choked. 'It's obvious that can't have been true!'

'There are different ways of being elusive. Erin——'

'Please!' She stood up. 'I have to leave.' She put the glass down. 'But not through there,' her voice broke emotionally, 'I couldn't face all those people again. Do you have a side-door I could leave by?'

'Yes. But——'

'Could you please show it to me? I have to get out of here.'

'I can't let you leave like this——'

'You can't stop me,' she choked.

'At least let me get someone to drive you home? Please, Erin, I would feel better if you did.'

'All right,' she sighed. 'But please make it quickly.'

'Two minutes,' he promised.

How could Josh have done this to her! He had told her he couldn't do the painting, that somehow it wouldn't come together. He had lied to her! He had painted her in minute detail, even down to the silvery scar left by her appendix operation as a child.

'Erin.'

She spun round to confront Josh. 'I'm leaving,' she told him abruptly. 'Matthew is getting someone to drive me home.'

'Me.' He quietly closed the door behind him, instantly shutting out the noise of the party.

'You?' she blinked. 'But——'

'I'm going to drive you home,' he told her quietly.

'No!' She shook her head, looking at him with tear-filled eyes.

Josh shut his eyes as if to shut out pain. 'I can't believe this is happening,' he groaned.

'Neither can I,' Erin said bitterly.

He put a hand up to his temple as if it ached. 'Matt said you believe I painted you out of lust, to hurt you.'

'Well, didn't you?' she accused.

'Of course not. You know how I feel about you——'

'So do all the people out there,' she waved her arm in the direction of the gallery. 'The whole world will know by tomorrow!'

He sighed. 'That was the idea.'

'I'm sure it was,' she snapped. 'Joshua Hawke, the great lover,' she scorned.

'I wasn't so great with you, was I? You couldn't even look at me afterwards.'

Colour flooded her pale cheeks. 'And all you could do was say you were sorry!'

'What else could I do?' he rasped. 'I would have got down on my knees and apologised, begged your forgiveness, if I thought it would do any good, if I thought it would change anything, but it was too late for that.'

'Much too late,' she agreed bitterly.

He turned away. 'Hell, I gambled everything on that painting. I thought it would tell you—show you——'

Erin frowned, not understanding the raw pain in his voice. 'Show me what, Josh? Tell me what?' she asked sharply.

He sighed, shaking his head. 'You remember I couldn't paint you? Well, after I'd made love to you I realised why.'

'Lust!' she dismissed scornfully.

'No,' he denied angrily. 'You see, I kept working on the face first—I daren't trust myself to paint your body,' he added ruefully. 'And I found it impossible to paint your face. There's no one expression I love the best, no way I could paint the face of the woman I loved, because I love every feature, every smiling, scowling feature. Even now the painting doesn't quite have features.'

'Josh, I'm not understanding any of this,' she shook her head. 'Are you saying you *love* me?'

'You know damn well I do!'

'No——'

'Of course you do,' he scowled.

'No—I—How long have you loved me?'

'For ever, I think,' he groaned.

'Seriously, Josh,' she said breathlessly.

'I am being serious. I can't remember a time when I *didn't* love you.'

'When we made love——'

'*God*, how I loved you then! And you hated the sight of me. I'd been fighting making love to you for days, that's why I had to spend so much time in the studio, and when you came to me that night I just couldn't fight any longer. I wanted you, I loved you, I had to have you. I couldn't stop myself.'

'But I didn't want you to. Josh, I—I love you

too. I have for weeks.'

He searched her eager face disbelievingly, his hands coming out to grasp her shoulders. 'You wouldn't be playing with me, would you?' he asked tentatively.

'Never,' she shook her head, her gaze locked with his. 'I loved you that night too, I loved you before then. But even when we were—well, even then you didn't mention loving me,' she blushed prettily.

'Neither did you.'

'But I—Well, I was afraid.'

'So was I.'

Her eyes widened. '*You* were?'

Josh gave a rueful smile. 'I've never been in love before, I didn't know how to handle it.'

She gave him a shy look beneath lowered lashes. 'We've been fools, haven't we?'

'It's beginning to look like it.' Some of the tension started to leave him. 'You really love me?'

'Very much.'

'And you'll marry me?'

'Oh yes!' Her eyes glowed.

'Oh God, Erin,' he groaned into her throat, his arms shaking as he held her against him. 'I love you!'

An office might not be the ideal place to give and receive a proposal of marriage, but the comfortable armchair Erin had occupied earlier was ideal for accepting the invitation, their murmured words of love and adoration interspersed with heated kisses.

At last Josh pulled back with a ragged sigh. 'When Matt told me you hated the picture I thought I'd lost you for ever.'

She nuzzled into his throat. 'I only hated it because I thought you'd painted it to mock me.'

'Never!' His arms tightened about her. 'After the fire I daren't let you come back to the bungalow. You seemed ashamed of the fact that we'd made love, and I couldn't trust myself not to touch you, to want you again, so I left you with Martha and Jim, and spent the time painting you.'

'Jim said you were helping to clear the damage caused by the fire.'

'I was, in the day. And at night, when I couldn't sleep for wanting you with me, I painted you.' He shrugged. 'It was all I had. But, believe me, I would rather have had you with me.'

'I thought you'd been disappointed in me, that you regretted what had happened.'

'When I've been wanting to do it again ever since?' he groaned.

'Josh!' She buried her face against his chest.

He gave a throaty chuckle. 'Well, I have.'

Erin looked up at him. 'When did you really fall in love with me?'

He shrugged. 'I don't know. I didn't like that Johnston guy touching you, I was even jealous of your liking Dave. And when you told me Bob had been your stepfather and not your lover I was so damned happy I felt like shouting.'

'You didn't act it,' she recalled dryly.

'Not straight away, no,' he gave a rueful smile. 'I had to stand under the cold shower for fifteen minutes to calm myself down. I also had to show you that you shouldn't have just gone off with a stranger like you did, not when you were an innocent. You could have landed yourself with anyone,' he frowned.

Erin smoothed that frown away with her fingertips, kissing him lovingly on the lips. 'Not anyone, darling. I'd already decided that I wanted to give my virginity to you. In the end I gave it to the man I wanted to marry, like you told me to.'

'And I thought you were ashamed.'

'When I loved you so much?' She shook her head. 'I was never ashamed in the way you mean. And like you, I've been wanting to do it again ever since.'

He groaned. 'I wonder if we could sneak out of here without anyone knowing?'

'I don't think so,' she laughed. 'Besides, I want everyone to see the original of the painting.'

Josh looked at her with concerned eyes. 'Are you sure? I can have it taken down—'

'Don't you dare!' she warned, knowing now that it had been painted out of intense love.

'Erin, you're sure you'll be able to take being my wife?' asked Josh. 'You've seen what it's like. I live like a recluse most of the time, and the rest of the time it's like this, being hounded by the press——'

'Which reminds me,' she interrupted sternly. 'Who was that glamorous brunette you were with the other night?'

He grinned. 'You wouldn't be jealous, would you?'

'Insanely!'

'You needn't be,' he chuckled. 'I wasn't even with her, she just happened to be standing next to me when the photograph was taken. I only went to the party because Matt said I should. I left about ten minutes later. I was so damned worried about you I couldn't think of anything else. When I found you'd gone, just disappeared ... I don't even want to think about it,' he shuddered.

'Oh, darling!' She kissed him passionately on the mouth, her lips parting invitingly as he deepened the kiss.

It was the sound of exaggerated throat-clearing that finally broke them apart. 'I hate to break up the—er—party,' Matt smiled, 'but the press would like a statement from you, Josh.'

'Then they shall have one.' He stood up, Erin held firmly against him. 'Ready, honey?'

'Ready,' she nodded, stars in her eyes.

She didn't hear anything of what was said after Josh began his statement with 'Ladies and gentlemen, let me introduce you to the future Mrs. Hawke ...'

She looked up from her sewing as Josh came into the room, at once standing up to receive the passion of his mouth.

'My second nude completed,' he murmured against her lips.

'It really is finished?' she said excitedly. The painting of herself hung on the studio wall, where only her husband could gaze at it.

'Mm,' he teased her with light kisses on her mouth and throat.

'I'm not sure I approve,' she said with mock sternness. 'Naked females cavorting about your studio!'

Josh gave a delighted chuckle. 'That "naked female" fell asleep halfway through the sitting. I had to change her diaper and put her to bed.'

Erin gave a gurgle of laughter. 'Poor Amy, she doesn't understand that her daddy wants to paint her.'

'Did I remember to thank you for our daughter?'

Their daughter, Amy Sharon, was three months old now, with her father's jet-black hair, and eyes like blue-green lakes. And they both adored her, although after eighteen months of marriage their love for each other had only deepened.

'About a hundred times,' Erin nodded. 'But I like the way you say thank you.'

'So do I,' he growled, lifting her up into his arms. 'Why do you think I do it so often?'

'I have no idea,' she answered mischievously.

'Hussy!' Josh laughed, laying her down on the bed before hastily joining her, his mouth claiming hers in deep possession.

CALGARY—THE OLD AND THE NEW

Cow Town, Sunshine City . . . Calgary has numerous nick-
names, but call it what you will, it is one of the fastest
growing, most exuberant cities in North America.

Planted in the eastern foothills of the Rocky Mountains,
in Alberta, Canada, Calgary is relatively young. Only a
century ago, Blackfoot Indians hunted buffalo where
skyscrapers now soar. What was once an army barracks, a
handful of houses and a general store catering to local
cattlemen has become a bustling metropolis of 570,000—
and growing by leaps and bounds every year.

The reason is oil, an abundant resource in Alberta.
Today a great deal of money and the expertise of thou-
sands pour into Calgary to support the rising commerce
and industry.

Yet one of Calgary's greatest tourist attractions is a
colorful celebration of the city's "Wild West" past—the
Calgary Stampede. For ten days every July, tourists from
all over the world thrill to such rodeo exhibitions as steer
roping, bronco riding and chuck-wagon races, and partici-
pate in parties, parades and lots of high-spirited fun.

Calgary is an interesting mix of not-too-distant past and
exciting present; and perhaps nothing better reflects the
character of the city today than the sight of a cowboy
sporting a ten-gallon hat and driving a Cadillac!

Readers rave about Harlequin romance fiction...

"I absolutely adore Harlequin romances! They are fun and relaxing to read, and each book provides a wonderful escape."
—N.E.,* Pacific Palisades, California

"Harlequin is the best in romantic reading."
—K.G., Philadelphia, Pennsylvania

"Harlequin romances give me a whole new outlook on life."
—S.P., Mecosta, Michigan

"My praise for the warmth and adventure your books bring into my life."
—D.F., Hicksville, New York

*Names available on request.